Susanne O'Leary

Borrowed Dreams

BORROWED DREAMS
By Susanne O'Leary

Copyright © 2015 Susanne O'Leary

Cover and paperback formatting by JD Smith Design

Chapter 1

"Name?" the voice said over through the intercom.

"Daisy Hennessey," she replied, squinting at the blinding light.

"Stand in front of the camera, please."

Daisy let go of the heavy suitcase she had trundled through the dark alley after the taxi driver refused to continue. She turned to the CCTV camera so that her face would be clearly visible and blinked, waiting for further orders from the robotic voice. But there was complete silence as she stood there, shivering nervously despite the near-tropical warmth of the summer night. Hysterical laughter rose in her throat, and she supressed the urge to stick her tongue out at the camera. She pulled herself together as the silence continued. What was going on? She squirmed while she waited. Was this the right house? Yes, the discreet plaque on the wall said: Villa Alexandra. This was the right address. What if they didn't let her in? They had to. She had phoned them when she left Antibes and was instructed to take a taxi, which cost more than she could afford, but she had been promised a refund when she arrived. If they didn't let her in, she would have to find an affordable hotel room—close to impossible in Saint-Tropez at the height of the season. She couldn't go back to Antibes. She had burnt all her bridges there.

Daisy jumped as the steel gates started to open and the voice said, "Enter." She grabbed the suitcase and dragged it into a small courtyard, where a red Alfa Romeo was parked between the wall and the steps leading to a set of massive oak doors studded with metal spikes. The doors opened silently. Daisy managed to drag the suitcase up the steps and through the doors before they slammed shut behind her. Inside, she found herself standing in a huge hallway, bare except for a round table of wagon-wheel proportions, on which stood a gigantic urn with an array of artfully arranged flowers like something out of a Dutch sixteenth-century still life. Their pungent scent filled the air and tickled Daisy's nose. She sneezed. When she recovered, wiping her nose with the back of her hand, she heard the sound of heels clicking on the marble floor. A slim brunette carrying a bunch of papers appeared. She stopped when she heard the sneeze.

"Do you have a cold?" she asked.

"No. It was the flowers," Daisy explained. "I have a touch of hay fever. It's not contagious." She took a tissue from the pocket of her jeans and blew her nose. "Okay. I'm fine now."

"Good." The woman took a few steps closer to Daisy and held out her hand. "I'm Belinda Fforde-Power, personal assistant to the owner." She spoke with an upper-class British accent that sounded oddly studied, as if she had taken elocution classes or was acting in a Noël Coward play.

Daisy shook the woman's cool hand. "Hello. I'm—" She stopped and giggled. "But, of course, you know who I am."

Belinda Fforde-Power nodded. "Yes. Daisy Hennessey, the house manager."

"Fancy term for a house-sitter," Daisy remarked. "But I'll be minding the dogs and all kinds of other things too, right?"

"That's correct." Belinda started to walk away on her dangerously high heels, gesturing to Daisy to follow her. "Please come this way. I'll go through everything with you and then show you your room before I leave. And, of course, you have to meet the dogs."

Daisy dumped the suitcase and trotted after Belinda, wondering how it was possible to wear such a tight linen shift without creasing it. They walked across the hall and into another room as bare as the hall except for a desk with a laptop on it.

"Yes. The dogs," Daisy said to break the silence. "Looking forward to that. Ivan and…"

"Bess."

"Oh yes. Ivan is the Russian greyhound."

"Borzoi," Belinda said as she sat down at the desk.

"Bless you."

"I didn't sneeze. That's the correct name for a Russian greyhound."

"Oops. Sorry. Okay, Borzoi. And Bess is a bichon frisé. You sent me the photos. Beautiful dogs."

Belinda switched on the laptop. "They both have issues, though."

"Issues?" Daisy said.

"All kinds of traumas and personality flaws." Belinda pulled a stool from under the desk. "Here, sit down beside me so I can show you everything on the computer. How the house works, the schedule and all the security codes. When I leave, you'll be on your own. Apart from Olivier, of course."

"Olivier?" Daisy went around the desk and sat down beside Belinda.

"Housekeeper. Handyman. Gardener. He maintains the house and the grounds and cleans the pool. But you won't see much of him. He kind of melts into the background, if you know what I mean. No need to worry about him. Things just get *done*, you know?"

"I see," Daisy said. "Sounds like the perfect man. Useful, yet invisible. I like the idea."

Belinda ignored her and turned to the computer screen. "Right, let's go through this, have a quick look at the dogs, and then I can leave. I have to get to Geneva before morning."

Daisy was about to ask why but stopped herself. She would have received a bland answer. Belinda was obviously on some kind of schedule. In any case, it was getting late, and bed—any bed—seemed a very good idea. She stifled a yawn and concentrated on the instructions Belinda was issuing with machine-gun speed.

A 3D plan of a house came into view on the screen. Belinda ran the cursor through each room.

"On the ground floor, you have the hall, this study, the drawing room, dining room, den, library and the movie-screening room. Also a cloakroom off the hall and a guest room with en-suite bathroom and dressing room. There's a gym next door to that. As you can see, the drawing room and den both have doors leading to the terrace and the pool. The gardens are below, and you'll find the path to the private beach just off that. CCTV cameras are placed in all these areas except the guest room and the upstairs bedrooms. Olivier keeps an eye on the CCTV images from the security room just off the kitchen, which is here." The cursor wiggled on a vast space off the den area. "There's no need for you to worry about that."

"Phew," Daisy said. "I wouldn't know how to cope with such things."

"All you need to do, apart from minding the dogs, is take delivery of the new furniture and have the pieces placed according to the chart in the folder marked Furniture."

Daisy nodded. "Seems easy enough. But why are the owners having furniture delivered while they're away?"

"They've just bought this house. They have other business to attend to at this time," Belinda replied. "But let's go through everything. The dogs have a room to themselves just off the terrace, where you will find everything you need for their care. Instructions and the exercise schedule are all on the noticeboard just inside the door. They have their own shower and pool for cooling off in hot weather." Belinda paused and turned to Daisy. "I hope you understand the importance of following each dog's schedule. They get very neurotic if things aren't done the way they like it."

Daisy sighed. "The poor little pooches."

Belinda shot her a suspicious glance. "Quite," she said and turned back to the screen. "Now, upstairs, there are five bedrooms all with their own bathroom and terrace. The master suite is *here*…" The cursor wiggled again at a set of rooms. "But that's completely off limits to you, of course."

"Absolutely," Daisy said, feeling as if she should hold up a hand in a scout's-honour gesture to emphasise her response.

"Your room is at the end of the corridor. It's small but very comfortable."

"Great." Daisy stifled another yawn.

Belinda glanced at her. "Just the security codes and then I can go." She proceeded to go through a whole list of instructions and then pulled out a leather-bound notebook from a drawer and handed it to Daisy. "Here. All the codes are in it. Encrypted, of course. Put the notebook in the small safe in your room. The safe here in the office will remain locked at all times. Only I and the owners have the combination, in any case." She looked at the diamond-studded Rolex watch on her wrist and got up from the desk. "Now, just the dogs and then your room. I'm running a little bit late, so we'll have to hurry up."

Daisy followed her along a short corridor, glimpsing a vast room that lay in darkness through double doors: the drawing room, according to the plan she had just seen. Belinda clattered down a short flight of stairs and flung open a door to a huge bright kitchen with an array of state-of-the-art appliances, including not one but two fridges and two gas stoves, side by side. The background hum from the fridges and freezers filled the room with the atmosphere of the control room of a spaceship. But there was no time to reflect. Belinda had already raced through to a utility room, where she came to stop in front of a half door. She peered over it and was instantly rewarded by a series of barks and whines.

Daisy joined her and looked over the door into a room, softly lit by two wall-mounted lights. The dogs stood at the door, their barks intensifying when they saw Daisy. The little dog with white fluffy fur was more ferocious than the spindly borzoi.

Belinda took a step back. "Better not annoy them," she shouted above the din. "You can deal with them tomorrow."

Daisy looked at the snarling, growling, barking dogs and held up a hand.

"Stop!" she yelled. The sudden silence was nearly as startling as the deafening noise.

"Sit!" The dogs sat.

"Bed!" Daisy ordered, hoping they knew what that meant. They did. They both got up and padded to their individual beds lined up along the far wall and lay down with a collective sigh.

"Good dogs," she said in a softer voice, astonished by their response to her commands, and closed the door.

Belinda's mouth closed slowly. "How did you *do* that?"

"Do what? Oh, the dogs." Daisy shrugged. "Haven't a clue. They were annoying me, so I told them so shut up, that's all."

Belinda still looked awestruck. "You must have some kind of gift."

"If I do, this is the first time I've used it."

Belinda nodded and checked her watch again. "Must get going. Do you think you could find your room on your own? It's very easy. It's the last one along the corridor to the left of the upstairs landing."

"Of course," Daisy said, relishing the idea of being on her own and being able to sink into a bed and go to sleep. "I used to be a girl guide. I have a very good sense of direction."

"Perfect. Well, I wish you the very best of luck. If you have a problem, you can e-mail me."

"Okay. Hopefully I won't." A thought struck Daisy. "The owners...who are they?"

But Belinda had left, the sound of her heels echoing down the corridor and across the marble floor of the hall. Daisy walked after her, hearing the front door slam in the distance. She was on her own.

After collecting her suitcase and lugging it up the wide stairs, Daisy arrived at a large upper landing and started to walk down the corridor as instructed. She came to a door and opened it, feeling for the light switch on the wall. When she found it, the room suddenly sprang into view. Daisy blinked and stared. Was this the 'small but comfortable' room Belinda had described?

The big room, furnished in Provençal style, was like an illustration from a brochure for luxury homes, with a terracotta-tiled floor and a big bed with an array of brightly coloured cushions piled high on the white cotton bedspread. The walnut side tables and rattan chairs added to the elegant look, and the curtains, swaying gently in the soft night breeze, were made of silk with an exquisite design of birds and flowers.

As Daisy padded around the room, she discovered a door leading to a walk-in wardrobe and another that opened into a bathroom with blue tiles and a bathtub the size of a small swimming pool. The shelves were piled with fluffy towels and rows of beauty products by Dior, Chanel and Yves Saint Laurent.

Daisy let out a whistle. Gee, if this was how the staff lived, what did the master's quarters look like? A sneak peek was definitively in order very soon. She took off her sandals and padded to the French window that opened onto a small terrace. The room overlooked the silent garden and the vast infinity pool, from which a soft whirling sound could be heard. She leaned on the railing and looked out to the sea glinting in the distance. The stars glimmered in the black sky, and high above them she could see the white swathe of the Milky Way. What a magical place. So still and silent despite the proximity of the nightclubs and restaurants of one of the most fashionable towns on the Riviera.

Daisy looked up at the stars. Was *he* looking at them, too? Maybe wondering where she was? She should have said goodbye. But she had to put distance between them for a while. The past months had been stressful and emotional. She needed time and space. That's why she had jumped at the chance of this strange job. House-and-dog-sitting in a luxury pad seemed like a very good idea. This way, she could disappear and live in this fortress without having to travel more than ninety kilometres. Peace and solitude. The best remedy for a troubled mind.

Chapter 2

Ever since her early twenties, Daisy had been drawn to bad men. 'Bad' in the sense that they were rude and insensitive. Sexy, yes. Good-looking, yes. Funny in a nasty way, yes. This had led to many, brief, hot affairs that ended in painful break-ups. After a particularly heart-breaking end to a relationship with one of those men, her mother had shaken her head and told her that one day, she would meet a nice man—'nice' meaning gentle, sensitive, warm, kind and loving—and she would fall in love with him. But it hadn't happened.

Daisy's romantic résumé was crammed with useless, lying, mean men, including several episodes of unrequited obsessions with men who simply didn't care about her. The kind of men who told her she would have been 'quite nice-looking with bigger breasts' or who would give her money for her birthday in a brown envelope as a kind of afterthought. Or who didn't give her anything at all. She was beginning to believe there was something wrong with her, which was confirmed when she met Ross. He was exactly the kind of man her mother said she would meet one day and think he was hot. He was sweet, kind, gentle, considerate and generous. Everything she should have loved. Except she didn't. Oh, she was fond of him, who wouldn't have been? And he was good-looking in that clean-cut Ivy League way: tall, blond, with blue-green eyes and a beguiling smile. He was intelligent too. And, of course, rich.

"Perfect, right?" she had said to Flora, who had agreed. "But not for me." Daisy sighed. "I just don't find him hot." She had ignored Ross' little hints and attempts at flirting and made him understand all she wanted from him was friendship. She felt a little guilty when she saw his disappointment and realised she was being utterly selfish. That way, she could stay in the stormy relationship with Bruno and keep Ross on the side as a friend—or security net, which was exactly what he turned out to be that night when she hastily filled two suitcases with her things and called him.

* * *

It all started the day Bruno asked her to get out of the apartment. Not because they were breaking up or had even had a row, but, as he explained, his grandmother wanted to let it to a friend who could pay a higher rent.

"But I can pay more if I find another roommate," Daisy argued. "The new girl at the agency might be looking—"

"No. My grandmother wants it for her friend," Bruno said, with a cool look in his eyes. "And she wants you to be gone by the end of the week."

"Where am I going to find a flat at such short notice?" Daisy asked, panic rising in her chest.

He shrugged. "You work in real estate. I'm sure you'll find something. Or someone might take you in temporarily."

"I'm not moving in with you."

"I don't think I mentioned that option. Why don't you ask your friend, Flora, if you can stay with her until you find something?"

"Flora's heavily pregnant with her second baby and lives over an hour's drive from here. I can't ask her. And don't say Chantal might offer me accommodation in her bijou apartment, either. She and Gabriel have finally moved in together and wouldn't welcome me playing gooseberry."

Daisy looked back at him, sitting there at the table on her terrace in the early evening light. So handsome, so sure of himself and her love. Sure of the total submission she had to show in order for him to stay in their relationship. So sure she would never jeopardise it by arguing. But he was trying to get her to leave an apartment she loved, where she had lived for nearly five years and now called home. They had been together for two of those years but not *living* together, at her request. He had agreed. It was better to live apart. She realised then why she never wanted to live with him. He was a control freak who lacked any empathy whatsoever. Sexy, yes. Drop-dead gorgeous, yes. Amazing in bed, yes. Funny and intelligent, yes. He ticked a lot of boxes except the most important ones.

Slowly taking off the rose-coloured glasses she had been wearing mentally ever since they met, Daisy got up from the table. She suddenly wanted to be as far away from him as possible. And she had just come up with an idea.

"Okay," she said. "I'll go. I'll start packing tonight. I'll take the day off tomorrow and do the rest, and then I'll be gone by tomorrow evening. Will that be fast enough for your granny?"

He looked slightly shell-shocked. "So soon? What are you going to do?"

"Do you care? I'm leaving this flat and our so-called relationship. That's what you were after, wasn't it? You're too much of a coward to just break up with me. You had to push me over the edge so I'd finally snap."

He got up. "That's not true. It was my grandmother who told me to—" He stopped and reached out his hand. "Ah, Daisy. You're so pretty. But we don't have much in common. It was fun, though, wasn't it?"

She backed away, trying to hold back the tears that were welling up in her eyes and strangling her voice. "Yes, at times, it was. I just wish I hadn't put any emotional investment into it. That I hadn't *cared* so much." She bent her head. "Please, just go. I don't want to talk to you. No discussions or arguments. There's no point. Let's just say goodbye and then I'll be gone."

She flinched as he touched her shoulder. "Goodbye, Daisy."

Then he was gone. She could start rebuilding her life and see if she could find a place to rest before she started the long road to recovery. She had no family, and most of her friends weren't in a position to help. Except one very special friend. She knew he would have been more than willing to offer her temporary accommodation. She dialled his number.

* * *

He was there instantly to pick her up. Knowing Bruno was watching from the window of his grandmother's apartment, Daisy fell into Ross' arms and kissed him long and hard on the lips. They loaded her bags into his vintage Land Rover and drove the short distance to his beautiful house, high on a hill on Cap d'Antibes. The glint of anticipation in Ross' eyes all through the rest of the evening made Daisy feel guilty. That kiss had promised more than she was going to deliver. But he didn't act on it straightaway. He helped her get all her stuff into the house and gave her the best guest room— the one overlooking the Bay of Angels—where Gabriel had painted Chantal over two years earlier. It had a beautiful en-suite bathroom with a roll-top bath, in which you could lie in hot water and look out over the bay, which was exactly what Daisy had done that night. The view of the velvety night sky and the bay with the lights along the Promenade des Anglais dotting the shore like a row of bright diamonds didn't quite register as she lay there, trying to recover from the shock and the hurt of having been rejected yet again.

What was wrong with her? Why did she always fall for these jerks? Was it some kind of kinky desire to be abused? No, that wasn't it. The thought of being physically abused by a man made her shudder. And Fifty Shades of Grey and any of the other spin-offs were sick and nasty. What was it, then? A bad self-image? Or the feeling she could tame a bad man? Maybe she felt flattered by the attentions of someone with this kind of sneery attitude, someone who was arrogant and mean but still attracted to her? Probably all of that rolled into one. And of course, she found them sexy. Daisy sighed and gave up the self-therapy. No use dwelling on it. She decided then and there to stay away from men for a while—maybe forever.

The following day, she and Ross spent a few hours wind-surfing. But the wind dropped and they ended up lying on the beach, talking.

Ross lay back on his beach towel and closed his eyes. "Great day. Except for the wind. But hey, it's summer so what can you expect?"

Daisy, who had just come out of the water, lay down beside him on her towel. "I love the way you just accept everything. Do you never bitch and complain?"

He opened one eye. "What's the point? I'm not into howling at the moon. Been there, done that. In any case, right now I'm quite content. I've managed to sort most of the problems of my life." He touched her hair. "Except my love life."

She turned her head to look at him. How had such a good-looking man escaped being caught by some nice girl who would have loved to look after this truly nice guy?

"What about your love life?" she asked. "In the past, I mean. What's your story there?"

He closed his eyes again. "Nothing to write home about. I've had precisely two serious relationships, but both ended because of my lack of trust." He paused for a moment. "Being wealthy brings a fear of being loved only for your money. And if you add my dislike of being a celebrity to that, plus my total lack of interest in fashion or the latest trends, you have a cocktail that few girls like for long."

Daisy sat up. "What? A good-looking guy with megabucks? I should think those two things would be all you'd need to catch a gorgeous woman."

"Superficially, yes. But not if you're looking for something really special. And I am."

"What are you looking for exactly?"

Ross looked at Daisy through half-closed eyes. "Comparability," he said after a long pause. "Commitment. Mutual respect. Don't ask me what I mean."

"I don't have to." The atmosphere between them had suddenly lost its light-heartedness. Daisy sprang to her feet. "I'm hungry. Let's have lunch somewhere really nice. Like the posh restaurant at the club on La Garoupe beach. Costs a fortune and I have no money, but you do."

"Gold-digger."

Daisy laughed. "Yeah, that's me. Come on, rich guy, take me to lunch. I need cheering up."

"We're not dressed for that kind of thing."

"Ah, come on, just flash your American Express platinum at them and they'll give us a table."

Ross scrambled to his feet. "How do you know I have one?"

"Just a wild guess."

"I don't. I have a Visa card and that's all. I like the simple life. Why can't we have a pizza at that restaurant over there?"

"But I've been there a million times. Oh, come on, Ross. I want to see how the other half lives. I need cheering up."

He scrambled to his feet and brushed the sand off his behind. "Okay, your Ladyship, but don't cry when they refuse to admit us." He pulled on his polo shirt and stuck his feet into his Docksiders. "You need to look as if you can at least afford their lobster salad."

"Lobster salad." Daisy sighed. "Sounds divine. I bet it's served with that fresh, crusty bread and their home-made mayonnaise. Can we have a glass of crisp white wine too?"

"Sure. If we manage to get past the maître d'. I've heard he's very snooty."

Daisy looked Ross over. "You know what? The way you dress whispers money ever so discreetly. I know, you're going to say you're scruffy, but a Ralph Lauren polo shirt teamed with those Yves Saint Laurent shorts and Docksiders, even if they are scuffed, is so that old-money-I-don't-give-a-damn look. And any snooty maître d' knows it."

"If he lets us in, he'll do it because he can't take his eyes off you. That bikini sits very well on your hot body."

Daisy pulled a pink linen shirt over her head. "He won't see my body. But I think I might be able to get past him. I know how to get around nasty men." She brushed her hair with her hand. "If I were still platinum blonde, it might have been easier."

"I love your real colour." He reached out to touch her hair. "It's like honey with blonde highlights. Goes with your lovely brown eyes."

Daisy pulled away. "Now don't get all smoochy on me. Come on, let's go and join the idle rich."

They arrived at the beach club just after the lunch rush hour and joined the last of the queue at the reception desk. The maître d', a tall dark man, looked down his thin nose at them.

"Have you booked?" he asked in French.

"No," Ross replied in English. "We were hoping you might have a table for two still free."

The maître d' sighed theatrically. "Reservations only, I'm afraid. Besides, this is a very expensive restaurant."

Daisy pushed herself in front of Ross. "We know. But we can afford it, believe me."

"That's not the problem," the maître d' replied. "We only accept guests who have reserved."

Daisy looked past him, down the steps to the terrace, where, in the shade of huge palms, sleek, sophisticated men and women sat at tables covered in white linen. There was a murmur of voices, the odd laughter and clinking of glasses, which, added to the delicious smell of food wafting in the light breeze, mingled into what Daisy had always thought of as the glossy world of the rich. She was like a poor little girl with her nose pressed against a shop window, looking at toys she couldn't have. She could hear Ross say something. She turned to him.

"Pardon?"

"I said we'll go to Eden Roc instead for lunch. I think the service is better there."

She stared at him. Eden Roc was possibly the most exclusive hotel on the Riviera. Why did he want to go there? Then she realised what he was doing.

"Yes, you're right," she drawled. "They have better food too."

The maître d' cleared his throat and looked Ross and Daisy up and down again until he seemed to spot something. Daisy followed his gaze. Ross' watch. That vintage rare Patek Philippe he had inherited from his grandfather.

"Just a moment," he said. "I think we have a cancellation." He took two menus from the desk. "Follow me." He trotted down the steps and started to weave between the tables, Daisy and Ross behind him, and then came to stop at a table just on the edge of the terrace, where the view of the water and the beach was superb. He flicked his napkin over the table, brushing away invisible crumbs and pulled out a chair for Daisy.

"Voilà, mademoiselle." Then he snapped his fingers at a waiter, bowed, wished them a pleasant lunch and left.

Slightly dizzy, Daisy blinked and stared at Ross. "You're a genius."

Ross pulled out his chair and sat down. "You just have to

play a blinder now and then. I didn't care whether he'd let us in, and I think he could sense that."

"Brilliant."

"I did it for you."

"I know." Daisy avoided his eyes and opened the menu, only to be able to hide behind it. There he was again, being so sweet and considerate. And she was using him.

The lunch continued in a very pleasant manner. Daisy ordered the famous lobster salad, and Ross had grilled sardines on a bed of baby spinach. They each had a glass of white wine, then champagne ice cream, coffee and petits fours to follow. The waiters fussed around them, serving fresh bread, brushing away breadcrumbs, pouring iced water into their crystal tumblers, removing plates and replacing them with new ones. The soft breeze brought with it a smell of the sea that mingled pleasantly with the slight whiff of garlic, herbs and newly baked bread. Daisy sighed happily. This was heaven.

She looked around at the other guests and noted the discreet elegance of the women and the studied casual dress of the men. They all had that rarefied air of effortless glamour and chic. You probably had to be born with it to be able to ooze that amount of confidence. She looked at Ross watching a windsurfer far away at sea, struggling with the slack winds. Although slightly bored, he looked at home there too, with his worn but expensive clothes, his patrician bearing and good looks.

Ross turned to her. "Sorry, I was looking at that wind-surfer out there and wondering if the wind will pick up. I think it will, the forecast said so. Do you want to go back to the beach?"

Daisy folded her napkin and put it on the table. "No. I think I'd like to go back to the house for a while. Maybe have a swim in the pool. Would that be all right?"

"Of course." He gestured at a waiter and asked for the bill.

After he had paid, Ross rose and pulled out her chair. "You don't have to ask. I want you to feel at home. I want you to be happy there."

"I am. But it's your home and I'm just a guest. I don't want to take things for granted."

He put his hand briefly on her shoulder. "I've never thought of you as a guest, Daisy."

His touch felt comforting, like that of a brother, but she knew he felt something different. She started to walk towards the entrance and his hand fell. Daisy was going to say something, but as she spotted a couple at a table near the steps, she froze to the spot.

"What's the matter?" Ross asked. "You look so pale all of a sudden."

"Look over there. Who do you see?"

Ross looked. "Shit, it's your ex-boyfriend. Didn't expect him to come to a place like this."

"He wouldn't," Daisy muttered. "He can't afford it." She looked at the woman opposite Bruno. "I've never seen that woman before. She looks rich, though. Look at the diamond bracelet and the Dior handbag. I bet she's paying."

Ross pulled at Daisy. "We can go out the other side and take the steps to the beach and—"

But Daisy wasn't listening. She marched over to the table and stopped, smiling at a startled Bruno. "Hi! Fancy bumping into you in a place like this."

Bruno's face took on a deep shade of red. "Bonjour," he mumbled and wiped his mouth with his napkin. "Nice day, isn't it?"

"Fabulous," Daisy purred. She turned to the woman, a heavily made-up blonde. "Hello, there. Hope you're enjoying your lunch."

The woman smiled politely. "Yes. It's lovely," she said in good but accented English.

"And how about your new apartment?" Daisy enquired

sweetly. "I'm assuming you just moved in. Are you enjoying that too?"

"How did you know?" the woman asked. "But yes, it's wonderful. The view from the terrace is—" She stopped, looking confused. "How do you two know each other?"

"It's complicated," Daisy said with a glance at Ross, who was looking increasingly uncomfortable. "Right, Bruno, baby?"

"Er…" Bruno said and coughed. He darted a glance full of hatred at Daisy. "I think you should leave now."

"Yes. I'm on my way." Daisy was about to turn on her heel when she spotted the carafe of iced water on the table. Fired up by a searing rage, she grabbed the carafe and emptied the contents over Bruno's head. Then she ran out of the restaurant with Ross at her heels.

He caught up with her in the parking lot, where she stopped at his car and burst into tears.

He took her in his arms. "Don't be sad, Daisy. That jerk isn't worth your tears."

Daisy buried her face in his shirt that smelled of soap and the sea. "I know. But I loved him so much. And then he humiliated me." She started to sob uncontrollably, shaking with grief and hurt. Ross tightened his arms around her and held her tight. Daisy felt herself relax into his warm embrace. It was so good to hug him like this, to feel the warmth of his body, know he truly cared and was sad for her, too.

"Come on, I'll take you home," he whispered.

She nodded, wiping her face on his shirt. "Yes, please." She touched his chest. "I've soaked you."

It'll dry." He pulled a rumpled but clean handkerchief from his pocket. "Here, blow your nose."

"Trust you to have a clean handkerchief when a girl needs it most." Daisy half laughed through her tears. "I'm sorry if I embarrassed you. We can never go back to that place."

"Who'd want to? I only went there because you were

so keen on it. I was delighted to see you drench that creep in iced water. Made him look really stupid. I couldn't help laughing."

Daisy laughed and blew her nose. "I didn't look. I just wanted to get out of there before I was arrested."

They got into the Land Rover and drove the short distance to Ross' house. After changing into a clean shirt, Ross prepared to leave for the beach. Daisy went to the pool, stripped down to her bikini and was about to get into the cool blue water when Ross joined her.

"Try to relax," he said and pulled her close. "I'll be back for dinner. I'll get a couple of steaks for the barbeque on my way home." Before she could protest, he kissed her, running his hands down her naked waist.

She pulled away. "No, Ross, please. I don't want you to think—"

He didn't seem to understand her discomfort. "We'll take it nice and slow," he murmured in her ear. "Go with the flow, see how we feel and where we want to go next. No pressure, no demands, just you and me doing what comes naturally."

He left before she could find the words to tell him that whatever he was hoping wouldn't, *couldn't* happen. She sank into the water and floated there, staring up at the sky, wondering how she could avoid sleeping with him.

* * *

Flora called while Daisy was relaxing in the shade beside Ross' pool.

"What happened to you?" she demanded. "You know I'm on maternity leave, but Chantal just called to say you've left."

"I—oh, Flora, I wasn't going to bother you. Yes, I did quit my job at the agency. I didn't get on with the new girl. But it wasn't just that. I've been planning to leave for a while. I want to do something else. Maybe get a job in a boutique or something. But that's not my biggest problem. I broke up with Bruno last night."

"You did? Good for you. Never understood why you were with him in the first place. Not a nice man."

"I know that now. He showed his true colours to me last night. He also threw me out of my apartment."

"How could he do that?" Flora asked. "His grandmother owns it. She'd have to give you at least a month's notice."

"She needed it for a friend, Bruno said. They would have allowed me to stay another month, but I couldn't stand the thought of it after our row. In any case, the story turned out to be a big fat lie unless his grandmother's friend is a bimbo with huge boobs."

"Holy mother. He's been cheating on you, too?"

Daisy felt tears well up. "I suppose he has. Anyway, I could have stayed another few weeks but I couldn't bear it. So I packed up my stuff and called Ross, and he came and picked me up straight away. So here I am, in his house."

"Ah. Okay. Ross must be happy, then."

"He is, but I'm not. He seems to expect…well, you know. And I just can't. I mean I could, but I don't feel like that about him. You know that. He's like a brother to me."

"Is that such a problem?" Flora started to laugh. "Listen to yourself. 'This great-looking rich guy is in love with me,'" she simpered. "'What am I going to dooo?' He'd marry you in a heartbeat and then you'd be rich, don't you realise that?"

Daisy sighed and giggled. "Yeah, I know. Sounds totally weird. I think I need therapy."

"Don't try me. I'm a lousy therapist. I'd just tell you to pull yourself together and get a life." Flora sighed. "But I do see your dilemma. What *are* you going to do?"

"I don't know," Daisy said bleakly. "I can't stay here for long. I have to find another place. Preferably far away."

"That might be the best solution. Where will you go? Back home?"

"No, I want to stay here. I love this area of France. I'll have to find a new job. I might go to Nice or Marseille."

"Maybe that would be best," Flora said. "But let me know where you are, if you do go."

"I will," Daisy promised. "Sorry for bothering you with my problems, Flora."

"I called you," Flora protested. "I wanted to know if you were all right."

"Well, now you know." Daisy mentally shook herself. What a wimp she was, sitting here in this stunning garden complaining about nothing. All she had to do was to get out of here and get a grip on her life. "I'll be fine. Don't worry. I'll call you in a couple of days."

"Great. Good luck," Flora said and hung up.

Daisy wandered back to the house and her room, where she changed into a fresh shirt and jeans. She had planned to unpack her suitcase, but changed her mind. No need to pretend to be moving in. A few days here and she would have to move on before Ross started coming to the wrong conclusions. But where would she go? Deciding to tackle that problem later, she went downstairs again and picked up the post on her way through the hall. She would read Le Figaro, catch up with the news and flick through the fancy Madame Figaro magazine that came with the weekend issue. She settled down on one of the white sofas in the living room. The awnings outside the windows had been lowered against the hot afternoon sun, and the large room was blissfully cool.

Daisy flicked through the magazine, studying the beautiful photos of amazing villas all over the Riviera. Some of them were truly magnificent, with infinity pools, terraced gardens, tennis courts and even private beaches. How incredible it would be to own something like that and have enough money to run it. Ross' house was lovely, but in no way could it compete with these Shangri La-like homes. She sighed wistfully and turned to the fashion pages and finally the advertisements at the back. She looked idly at ads for interior design services, household staff, nannies and gardeners. Nothing suitable there. She was going to close the magazine and turn back to the main paper, when a small notice at the bottom of the last page caught her eye: *House- and dog-sitter wanted for newly built villa in Saint-Tropez...*

Chapter 3

A ray of sunshine tickled Daisy's nose. She opened her eyes and looked around the dark room for a while, wondering where she was. Tiny specks of dust danced in the bright beam coming through a slit in the curtains. She realised she had forgotten to close the shutters before sinking into bed the night before. But she had been exhausted and in no fit state to do anything except close her eyes and go to sleep.

She peered at her phone to check the time. Half past seven. She couldn't remember the last time she had been up that early. She was such a night owl usually and never saw the point of being up with the lark.

A light breeze stirred the curtains, bringing with it the smell of freshly made coffee and newly baked bread. Daisy sniffed, feeling her stomach rumble. In her rush to get away, she hadn't eaten much the night before. Hungry and wide awake, she got out of bed, pulled open the curtains and walked into the bright sunshine, suddenly hit by the beauty of the early-morning light and the stunning view from her balcony. She had only glimpsed the garden and the pool in the moonlight and hadn't been able to take much of it in. She leaned on the railing and marvelled at the large terrace below and the infinity pool that looked as if it was suspended in thin air above manicured lawns that rolled all the way down to the seashore, where she could see the curve of a small bay with a white sandy beach fringed with palm trees. How heavenly it all looked, so pristine and new and untouched—which, of course, it was, having been newly built. Her eyes focused on the terrace, where a table had been set for breakfast under an umbrella. Who had set it? Possibly the mysterious Olivier. And was it for her? Daisy grabbed the white cotton wrap from the hook by the bathroom door and made her way along the corridor, down the wide staircase, through the vast, empty living room and through the French windows leading to the terrace.

She sat down at the table, sniffing hungrily at the basket of still-warm croissants and helped herself from the silver coffee pot. Sipping coffee and biting into warm flaky pastry, she felt as if she had strayed into a chapter of Alice in Wonderland. If there had been a sign on the croissants saying 'Eat me', she wouldn't have been a bit surprised.

She suddenly noticed an envelope with her name on it and a set of keys beside her plate. Inside, she found several pages of additional instructions and a note from Belinda.

Dear Daisy,

Please find enclosed the keys to the SUV you'll find parked in the garage in the basement. You can use it for shopping and getting around, but most importantly to take the dogs for their walks three times a day. They aren't allowed on the beach, but there are woods above Ramatuelle, where you can let them have a good run. They'll obey the dog whistle you'll find on the seat of the car. There's a remote for opening the garage doors and the gate in the glove compartment. Don't lose it. The dogs like to walk at around nine a.m., just before lunch and at eight o'clock in the evening. The rest of the time they'll stay in their room and the enclosed area outside it. Don't let them roam around the house. They're fed after their evening walk. Also, please read the instructions for the scheduled delivery of the furniture and where it's to be placed. Olivier will cook your meals according to the menus on the board in the kitchen. Please fill in your choices each morning and let him know if you don't plan to be in for lunch or dinner. He'll also do any shopping if you leave a list on the kitchen table. If you have any questions, e-mail me at the address I gave you last night.

 Best wishes,

 Belinda

Daisy stuffed the note and instructions back into the envelope and reached out for a second croissant but pulled her hand back. One was enough. No need to pile on the pounds. Her hips were still slim and she wanted them to stay that way; she didn't want to become a comfort eater. She glanced at her watch. Just after eight. There was plenty of time for a swim before she dealt with the dogs. Rising from the table with the intention of going back to her room for her bikini, she noticed a towel and a swimsuit hanging off the back of one of the loungers at the pool. Maybe it would fit her?

She walked down the steps to the lower terrace and took the swimsuit into the changing room of the little pool house. The interior was furnished with rattan chairs, a large mirror and a console, on which stood a crystal jug of water and an array of bottles containing sunscreen, body lotion and eau de cologne, all from top cosmetic companies, just like the beauty products in the guest bathroom. Daisy pulled on the light-blue swimsuit and found to her astonishment it was brand new and fitted her perfectly. She did a little twirl in front of the mirror, admiring the way the colour brought out her tan and hugged her curves, emphasising her tiny waist and slim hips. She shook back her hair, happy she had let it return to its natural dark blonde. The platinum bombshell look had been fun but this was more natural, more the real Daisy Hennessey from Brooklyn. She was slowly changing, slowly maturing, finding her true self. The escape from Antibes and the mess she had left in her wake seemed like a bad dream. Time to look forward and decide what to do next.

She walked back into the brilliant sunshine and, without hesitating, dived into the turquoise water of the pool. Surfacing, she broke into a crawl and did several laps before she stopped and rested her arms on the outer edge, looking out at the view and the bright azure of the sea far below. It all looked so perfect, as if it wasn't possible to feel sad or angry in such a setting.

She turned and looked to the left of the lawn, where she could see a high wall and the roof of the neighbouring house above it, sticking out over a copse of oleander bushes and small palms. Who lived there? The house looked older and smaller than Villa Alexandra. A window upstairs opened suddenly, and she could hear the morning news on someone's radio. A head appeared briefly and disappeared. Who was that? The owner? Or one of the servants? But it was time to take the dogs for their morning walk. Daisy swam to the steps and got out of the pool, had a quick shower and dried herself, mentally going through the instructions as she went back to her room and got dressed. Get dogs, find jeep and drive to woods. Seemed easy enough.

The dogs rushed forward barking and whining, when Daisy opened the top of the half door, Bess, the little bichon frisé, the most ferocious.

"Quiet!" Daisy yelled. The dogs stopped at once. She glared at them. "Behave yourselves or there'll be no walkies." The dogs whimpered. Ivan wagged his tail and sat. Bess lay down and rolled her eyes as if to say 'you're no fun'.

Daisy opened the bottom half of the door, took the leads and clipped them onto the collar of each dog. Then they both rushed ahead, Daisy hanging onto the leads shouting 'Heel!' to no avail. Her arms straining, she was dragged down the steps that led to the garage, where she found a red Porsche, a black Daimler and a green Volkswagen Touareg. The dogs stopped in front of it, scratching and whining.

Daisy groped for the key she had stuffed into the pocket of her shorts.

"Calm down. I have to open the door before you can get in."

She pressed the key and opened the door to the back and the dogs jumped in and settled, tongues lolling, looking as if they were smiling.

The drive to the woods was uneventful, up a steep road lined with scruffy cork oaks and pine trees. The road narrowed and they came to a stop at a dead end, where Daisy parked and let the dogs out. They both scampered along a path into the woods, Daisy following at a jog, grateful she had had the foresight to put on her running shorts and Nikes. She jogged on, hoping she would be able to catch up with the dogs when they had slowed down. She could hear them barking up ahead. Suddenly, they fell silent. Then a whine and a cacophony of barking and snarling. Something had frightened them. When she went around the bend, she saw what it was and froze. A wild boar sow with six piglets by her side stood snorting and pawing the ground, just in front of the dogs.

Daisy couldn't move. This was dangerous. Although the boar was not quite the size of a Labrador, it was twice as wide and sturdy, and she knew it could do serious damage with those impressive tusks. She also knew that sows with piglets were the most dangerous of all and wouldn't hesitate to attack if they felt threatened. And this one had to feel very threatened by two barking, growling dogs. Well, one to be precise, as Ivan backed away and tried to hide behind Daisy. Bess kept barking, curling back her lips and showing her teeth, her back rigid.

Daisy didn't quite know what to do. Trying to scare the animal away by shouting and waving didn't seem a good idea. If the dogs stopped barking, the sow was sure to attack them at once. And maybe the male was somewhere nearby?

Bess moved closer to the sow, which was now grunting and pawing the ground, her head down as if she was about to attack.

"No, Bess," Daisy whimpered, unable to move.

Suddenly, a shot rang out, echoing through the woods. Daisy jumped and screamed. The boar turned tail and ran, her squealing and grunting piglets following close behind. The ensuing silence was broken by the dogs' panting. Daisy's heart beat like a hammer in her chest, and she turned around slowly to face whoever had shot at the boar.

A man in jeans and a navy T-shirt stood there, a shotgun broken over his arm. His black hair was ruffled by the wind and his unshaven face was deeply tanned. He grinned, showing a row of white teeth.

"Bonjour, mademoiselle," he said in heavily accented French. "Ne vous inquiétez pas. Je ne suis pas dangereux. I'm not dangerous," he said in English. "Not going to shoot you, missus," he added with a wink.

"Jesus," Daisy breathed, her hand on her chest. "I nearly died of fright. What the hell are you doing here with that?" She pointed a shaking hand at the shotgun.

"You're American?"

"Yeah and you're a freaking Irishman. From County Cork if I'm not mistaken?"

"Yer not."

"Thought so."

And who are you? Apart from being American, I mean."

"None of your business."

He sighed and shook his head. "That's the thanks I get after saving your life?"

"Okay, thanks."

He peered at her. "How come you know so much about Ireland if you're from—wherever it is."

"I'm from New York," Daisy replied. "But I've spent a lot of time in Ireland. I have family there."

"He studied her for a moment. "But you look more French than Irish with those dark eyes."

"My mother's family came from Italy. My dad was from Dublin."

"Great mix. Have you been in France long?"

"Yes. Nearly five years."

He looked impressed. "You must be fluent in French by now."

She laughed. "Nah. Can't get my head around those irregular verbs. And the accent is a whore. But I muddle along as best I can, speaking 'Franglais' as the French call it."

His grin widened. "I bet you've had no complaints from the men, though," he said, scanning her body.

Daisy suddenly felt self-conscious. Maybe the shorts were a little—short? She tugged at them. Then, what he just said sank in and she shot him an angry look.

"Are Irish men generally that sexist? I thought Ireland had been dragged into the twenty-first century. 'No complaints from the men,'" she mimicked. "Gee, what was I supposed to do there? Blush and simper and say thank you?"

He coloured slightly and shifted the shotgun to his other arm. "Okay. Sorry. You're right. That was a little sexist, I suppose."

"More than a little."

He pointed at the dogs now gathered around Daisy as if needing reassurance. "Nice dogs. Are they yours?"

"Yes." No need to tell him any more about herself.

"I see. Do you live nearby?"

"You're very inquisitive."

"You're not going to tell me."

"You got it. But I might if you tell me what you're doing here in the woods with a shotgun."

"No, I won't." He grinned. "I think we're quits. Let's be mysterious."

Daisy nodded. "Good idea."

He gestured with his thumb over his shoulder. "That your four-by-four down there?"

"No. I stole it."

He snorted a laugh. "You're a gas girl. I bet the car belongs to your parents or something. And that the house you live in is pretty fancy."

Daisy suddenly felt he was standing too close. "Yeah, well, whatever."

He grinned "I'll take that as a yes."

He was standing so close, she could see the smile in his brilliant-blue eyes fringed with black lashes and that there was a tiny chip missing in one of his front teeth. He smelled of something clean and spicy. How attractive he was, like something out of an American thriller. But maybe he was dangerous? A hired killer on the run? A criminal wanted by the police?

She backed away. "I have to go."

"Me too. He lifted the shotgun. "Lots of shooting to do, ya know."

"I bet. Well, see you around or something," she said and skirted around him with the dogs at her heels.

"Nice to meet you," he called after her before he disappeared up the path.

When Daisy got back to the clearing where she had parked the SUV, she saw a dusty black Ferrari beside it. Could that have been his car? He didn't look as if he had a lot of money. But maybe he was an eccentric millionaire? What was he doing in the woods with a shotgun? It wasn't the hunting season and it was probably illegal to shoot anything in the summertime.

She got her explanation when she opened the back of the car to let the dogs in and spotted a sign she hadn't seen before. BALL TRAP, it said, which made her shake her head and laugh. Clay-pigeon shooting. That's what he was up to. There must have been a clay-pigeon club or something farther up the hill. Her theory was confirmed by the sound of a shotgun going off twice in rapid succession, and she could see a clay disc shatter against the clear blue sky. He was good at it, too. What else was he good at? Daisy smiled as she conjured up his image in her mind. No. Better not go there or even daydream. Men were trouble and she had had enough of that for a while.

* * *

Lunch had been set on the patio by invisible hands. Daisy sat down and helped herself from a platter of melon, ham, lettuce and thinly sliced cheese. She took a piece of bread and looked out over the quiet garden and the beach, where the water lapped the white sand. It would be nice to spend an hour or two with a book down there after lunch.

Her thoughts were interrupted by her phone ringing. When she answered, she heard a voice with an Italian accent asking, "Is that Daisy Hennessey?"

"Yes, that's me."

"Good afternoon. This is Giovanni Canova from Riviera Interiors in Cannes. Did Belinda mention us?"

Daisy swallowed the piece of bread she was chewing. "Yes, I think there was something about your firm in my instructions. You're in charge of the new furniture and the deliveries, is that right?"

"Correct. We'll be along at the end of the afternoon to supervise the installation of the living-room suite that's being delivered. It's coming from Milan, and they were just in touch to say they'd be there then."

"Okay. Looking forward to seeing you."

The afternoon seemed to be slipping away already. The dogs had to be taken for their afternoon walk around three, and then she had to be back for the arrival of the interior designer and the furniture. But it was only twelve thirty. Daisy decided to go down to the beach for a swim and a post-prandial rest. It was siesta time, after all.

After finishing her lunch, she was about to go to the kitchen and make herself a cup of espresso with the machine she had seen there before heading down to the beach. But before she had a chance to get up, she heard footsteps on the tiles behind her. Startled, she turned around and discovered a tall dark-skinned man in a white jacket, carrying a silver tray with a coffee cup, sugar bowl and cream jug. He had a somewhat regal bearing, despite his white servant's jacket.

He nodded at Daisy. "Bonjour, mademoiselle."

"Uh, bonjour," Daisy replied. "You must be Olivier."

"Yes." He placed the tray in front of her on the table and started to remove her plate and the platter.

"I'm Daisy."

"I know, mademoiselle."

"Thanks for lunch. It was delicious."

"You're very welcome, mademoiselle." Olivier nodded and walked away, carrying the debris of her lunch. He obviously didn't want to fraternise with her in any way. The discreet butler. How strange but at the same time exciting. She had never had a butler before. But then 'daughters of immigrant cleaning ladies didn't tend to have personal servants. He wasn't 'hers', strictly speaking; he belonged to the house, if 'belong' was the right word. Strange house. Strange owners who just disappeared immediately after buying it, leaving other people to set it up. Who were they? She didn't even know their nationality. Daisy suddenly felt a compulsion to explore the house. She hadn't seen much of it since she arrived the day before. But the beach beckoned, and the hot sun burning her back made her yearn for a swim in the cool blue waters of the sea.

The noise from the cicadas increased as Daisy walked

down the lawn and found the hidden path leading to the beach. The palm trees and shrubs provided a welcome shade, and she paused there for a moment before walking onto the hot sand. She looked out across the water. Someone was waterskiing farther out, cutting a swathe of white in the still blue surface of the sea. He was obviously very expert, doing all kinds of swerves and loops as the motorboat pulled him along at breakneck speed. Daisy watched him for a while, admiring his skill and athletic body. Some rich playboy, no doubt, who had been doing it since he was a child.

Longing to cool off, Daisy walked onto the scorching sand of the beach, regretting she hadn't taken her hat with her. But when she peered into the little beach hut she had spotted at the far end of the beach, she found a beach umbrella and a number of beach loungers stacked against the wall. There were also towels and a cool box, which, on further inspection contained chilled bottles of water, orange juice and beer. Olivier had obviously read her mind yet again.

Daisy unfolded the beach umbrella and pushed the end of it into the sand. After setting up one of the beach loungers under it, she quickly stripped off, put on her bikini, ran down to the water's edge and threw herself into the water. After floating for a while, she turned and swam in a slow crawl straight out into the bay, enjoying the cool water. Then she turned on her back and floated again, looking up at the blue sky. As she lay there, she felt the calming effect of being submerged in water, and she began going through the events just before her sudden departure from Antibes. Had it been the right thing to do? Maybe staying on and sorting things out would have been a more sensible approach? Talking it through with Flora or Chantal might have helped, but they had been busy with their own concerns at the time and in no position to take on other people's problems, even those of a close friend.

* * *

Feeling lost and alone and knowing she couldn't let Ross think he was anything other than a friend, the ad for this luxury house-sit she had found in the magazine seemed like it was meant for her. She applied at once by e-mail, taking care to include her phone number. The woman called very soon after that. It only took a short conversation, and after having e-mailed the references Chantal had given her, the job was hers.

By the time Ross had come back with the steaks and wine, she was nearly ready to leave. She was about to tell him but changed her mind. She didn't want to break his heart, didn't want another row. She would just leave when he was asleep. In any case, she was hungry.

Ross cooked the steaks on the barbeque, and Daisy made a salad and opened the wine. They sat under the large umbrella pine on the terrace, drinking wine and chatting until the sun set, and one by one, the stars twinkled in the dark-blue sky.

Ross looked across the table at Daisy. "Can't believe you're here, living with me."

"Not living," she protested. "I'm just staying with you until I find something else."

"Oh, whatever," he laughed and took her hand. "We'll take it slowly. That's what I promised and I'll stick to that. We've been friends for a long time. We know each other well. Isn't that a great start?"

"But I don't want that to end," Daisy said, her voice quivering. "If we get into something else, we might lose the friendship." She looked at his dear face in the dusk and knew she meant that. He was the best friend she had ever had. She pulled her hand away. "Please, Ross…"

He got up from his chair, and pulled her to him, holding

her by the arms and gazing into her eyes with a look so full of love it made her cringe.

"Don't worry, my Daisy, I would never want to force you into something you don't want. But you will want it, I'm sure of that. In the meantime…" He pulled her closer and kissed her deeply.

Without thinking, she kissed him back, only because it felt so good to be held close and to be loved. She put her hand on his chest and felt his heartbeat. Such a good heart. Strong, honest and true. Then she pulled away.

"Oh God, Ross, don't. I can't. I'm so fond of you, but—"

"But you liked that. I could tell. That was a pretty hot kiss for someone who just wants to be friends." He let her go. "Enough for tonight, or I'll have to break my promise. Goodnight, sweetheart. See you in the morning." He walked away into the darkness, his footsteps crunching on the gravel.

Daisy sat down again to finish her wine and to think. Time to go. Once Ross was asleep, she would leave.

She packed her bag quickly, and after pushing a note under Ross' door, she called a taxi and left without looking back. It was such a relief to leave, to cast off and escape the stress and heartbreak of her break-up with Bruno and the mix-up with Ross.

Dearest Ross, she thought, *will I ever meet you again? So honest and true. But I didn't deserve you, couldn't deal with your sweet concern. I didn't love you enough.*

Chapter 4

Her mind still lingering on that last day with Ross, Daisy wandered back up to the house to get the dogs for their afternoon walk. She gazed up at the villa. From there, it looked like a big white glass and cement cube hovering over the lawn. It had a futuristic look, like something out of a sci-fi movie, and she suddenly felt as if she were in a different dimension, a kind of twilight zone. She half expected aliens to come out on the terrace, and froze as she saw a figure dressed in white moving around up there. She shook herself and continued on. It was only Olivier cleaning the pool. But maybe he was some kind of other-worldly being? He didn't *seem* like the normal butler or servant. There was something odd about him; he had a kind of dignity and reserve, combined with a touch of mystery which was slightly unnerving. Where did he come from? He wasn't French, and he spoke English with an accent she had never heard before.

"Where do you come from, Olivier?" she asked when she reached the terrace.

"Eritrea, mademoiselle."

"I see. And do you have family there?"

"No, mademoiselle. They all died in the war."

"The war?"

"Yes, the war of independence against Ethiopia." Olivier put down the pole with the vacuum head at the side of the pool.

"I'm sorry. How sad."

"Yes." He inclined his head. "Thank you."

"Do you live here, in the house? I didn't see servants' quarters on the plan."

"They're on the lower ground floor. But I don't live there."

"Where do you live, then?"

"In town."

"Oh. Well, probably better than living in the servants' quarters," Daisy remarked. When there was no reply, she went on to the next thing that had been on her mind since she arrived. "The owners of this house…who are they?"

"I don't know, mademoiselle."

Daisy stared at him. "You don't? Not even where they're from?"

"No, mademoiselle." Olivier gathered up his pool-cleaning tools. "Will there be anything else?"

"No, thanks."

"Very well." Olivier glided away toward the kitchen.

Daisy threw back her coffee and followed him. The dogs had to be walked. But it was too hot for a good run, so she decided to take them on their leads across the lawn to a fenced-off area with rough grass she had spotted earlier.

"Is that little field accessible to the dogs?" she asked Olivier, when he had stored the tools in the utility room.

"Yes. It belongs to the property. I think it is supposed to be turned into a tennis court. You can take the dogs there when they only need a short walk. But you have to put their leads on and take a plastic bag to clean up after them. You'll find bags in the box beside their feeding bowls."

"Thanks." Relieved not to have to go for a long walk, Daisy fetched the dogs and took them to the field, where she let them off to shuffle around and do what they needed to do. It was much hotter than earlier, and they seemed happy to go back to their cool quarters, where they both had a long drink out of the marble trough. She left the door open. It seemed a little unkind to have them locked up all the time. Not familiar with dogs, she nevertheless felt these ones had been neglected and needed the company of humans. But the dogs didn't stir, looking as if they preferred to stretch out on the cool floor tiles of their own space.

The day stretched before her and the only excitement was the arrival of the interior designer and then the delivery of the furniture. Daisy went to the office to be ready to let him in once he rang the intercom. She had to check his ID before she opened the door. As she passed through the hall, she saw that the flowers had been replaced with fresh ones and the morning's post had been put on the large table. She picked up the pile. She was supposed to sort the mail, open anything that looked important and report back to Belinda if any of them needed a reply.

"It'll be mostly brochures and invoices," she had said. "And all the bills will have been paid by direct debit, so just file them in the folder on the desk. You can send regrets to any invitation by e-mail or post."

Apart from a few invoices, the pile contained two brochures and three invitations; all addressed to Monsieur et Madame Alexei Kedrov, Villa Alexandra, Saint-Tropez. Kedrov? That sounded Russian. Was that where the owners were from? Or were they simply Americans of Russian descent? She opened the invitations: a gallery opening, a drinks party at some villa in Ramatuelle and a fancy-dress party a week later. The RSVPs had e-mail addresses. She would send the replies later.

Daisy jumped as the intercom rang. She went to the CCTV screen, where the fuzzy picture of a woman with dark curly hair had just appeared.

"Name?" Daisy said into the mike, feeling suddenly powerful.

"Claudia Canova," the woman said, "from Riviera Interiors. I'm Giovanni's sister. He couldn't come so—"

Daisy hit the button to open the gate.

"Please come in," she said.

On closer inspection, Claudia Canova was a stunning woman in that Italian sexy way.

"Hi," Daisy said as she opened the door. "Come in. Sorry about the intercom. It's a bit scary."

Claudia laughed and nodded. "Si, si. Very scary. I thought you were a robot who'd shoot me if I didn't answer correctly."

"I know what you mean. I felt the same when I arrived yesterday." She held out a hand. "I'm Daisy. The house-sitter."

"Buon giorno, Daisy," Claudia said. Her handshake was firm and her eyes friendly. "It's very nice to meet you. What an amazing house." She took a clipboard out of her large tote. "I have the schedule here for the deliveries. Could you show me the living room?"

"It's this way." Daisy walked across the marble floor and continued down the corridor. "It's huge and empty. It'll be nice to see it furnished."

Claudia followed, her high heels clicking behind Daisy. Once in the vast living room she gasped. "Mamma mia! This is enormous. I haven't seen it before. Giovanni did the design for this one." She walked to the huge windows and looked out at the pool and the view beyond. "I've been in a lot of luxury villas on this coast, but this one has the best views."

"I know," Daisy agreed. "The house itself isn't pretty from the outside, but from here it's like being in some kind of spaceship."

Claudia nodded. "Yes. I studied architecture in London and I've done some similar designs but never on this scale."

"That explains your great English. So how come you're doing interiors and not designing houses?"

"The property market went into decline," Claudia explained, "so instead of setting up my own company, I joined my brother's firm that was already established here on the Riviera, and now we're doing up existing houses instead of building new ones."

"Sounds like a good idea."

"There is no shortage of rich people around here." Claudia peered at Daisy. "Who owns this house? I've only ever dealt with Belinda, who organised everything. But I've never spoken to the owners or even heard their name."

Daisy hesitated. Would it be safe to tell Claudia the name she had seen on the envelopes? Belinda hadn't left any specific instructions about that. Claudia looked responsible and trustworthy.

"They're called Kedrov. That's all I know. But I think they live in New York and have homes in other places too."

"Sounds Russian," Claudia remarked. "But they could be English or American or even French." She shrugged and consulted the Cartier Tank watch on her wrist. They'll be here to deliver the sofas about now. Then the artwork will be here a little later with some of the antiques and the floor covering, of course. They've commissioned a huge Aubusson rug especially for this room. Money is no object, it seems."

"No, that's becoming increasingly obvious."

The doorbell bell rang. Daisy went to open the gate and made sure it stayed open so the delivery truck could get in.

The next hour was taken up with deliveries and getting two huge white sofas in place in a L-shape in front of the windows. Then the rest of the furniture arrived and was placed with military precision following orders from Claudia.

The Aubusson rug, in hues of sage green and pale pink, was placed on the floor and the glass coffee table on top of it. Then the antiques arrived along with the artwork. Daisy recognised two of the large canvases instantly.

"That's by Gabriel Sardou. Part of his Bay of Angels series. I know it so well." She peered at the profile of the woman in the painting. "And that's Chantal, his partner."

"You know them?" Claudia asked. "That's fascinating. "Tell me more. I have a feeling there's a lot of amore between the artist and this woman, no?"

Daisy glanced at the two workmen busy hanging the paintings. "Not really. I just kind of know *of* them."

"Gabriel Sardou used to live in Saint-Tropez, but I've heard he's now based in Antibes."

Daisy nodded. "That's right. Chantal and he are...well, you know."

Claudia smiled and winked. "It's all right. No need to go into details. You want to be a little...discreet, I feel."

"Yes. Perhaps," Daisy said.

Claudia nodded and turned her attention to three large abstracts that were just being carried into the living room. She shouted instructions in Italian to the workmen, and it took some arguing before she was happy and the paintings were in place.

Only then did Daisy notice the last one that was hanging over the antique console. "That's a...Picasso!"

Claudia nodded. "Yes. But it's a copy. The original hangs in the owner's permanent home, Belinda told me. Wherever that is."

"They must be seriously wealthy, then."

"Very seriously," Claudia agreed with a laugh. She surveyed the room. "Well, that's the living room all ready. Looks nice, don't you think?"

Daisy looked around in awe. The cold, cavernous space had sprung to life. The walls adorned with the paintings that sparkled with vibrant colours and the floor covered in the soft Aubusson rug framed the subtle design of the furniture perfectly. The white sofas were embellished with embroidered cushions in bright colours, the antiques added to the elegance, and the huge windows were hung with linen curtains that stirred in the soft breeze.

"Absolutely stunning. You're a genius, Claudia."

Claudia laughed. "It wasn't me, it was Giovanni. He has a good eye for what suits a house, I suppose. You should see the bedrooms. They're fantastic. I've only seen the photos, so the real thing must be even better. And the master bedroom is fabulous, as far as I could tell." She stuffed her clipboard into her bag. "That's all for today."

"Do you want a drink before you go?" Daisy offered. "I'd love some iced tea myself. I can ask the butler to bring us some out on the terrace."

"Thanks, but not today. I have to get back to the office and sort out some invoices."

Daisy felt a pang of disappointment. It would have been nice to chat with this nice woman. Or anyone at all, really. The big house was already beginning to feel lonely.

"Of course. I understand," Daisy said and followed Claudia down the corridor to the hall and the front door. "Give me your mobile number and I'll put it onto my phone. I left it in the office."

"Perfect. I need you to sign the invoices for the deliveries today, anyway."

When Daisy had filed Claudia's number into her contacts and signed the forms, she picked up the pile of letters still on the desk. "Oh, shit, I forgot all about these. I have to sort them out and reply to the invitations."

Claudia glanced at one of the cards. "That's a drinks party I wouldn't mind going to. It'll be packed with famous people."

"Really?" Daisy looked closer at the card. "Very fancy, with the embossed text and all. Who are they?"

"A German millionaire and his third wife. She's Swedish and was a model before she married him. Their house is wonderful. Giovanni did it before I joined him. It's right on the waterfront."

"Sounds fabulous," Daisy sighed. "Would be fun to see it. Pity I can't go."

Claudia smirked. "But why can't you?"

"What?" Daisy stared at Claudia. "Go? To the party? But it's addressed to Mr and Mrs—"

Claudia laughed. "I was joking! Of course you shouldn't. I mean, yes, it would be possible to go there and flash the card at the security guard at the gate. He wouldn't check that carefully and wouldn't know what the real Mrs—what was that name again?"

"Kedrov."

"Yes. They wouldn't know what the real one looked like. Nobody knows them around here yet. They just bought the villa and then left, leaving Belinda in charge of everything. And now she's in Switzerland. So if you had the nerve to fake it, you could."

Daisy laughed and shook her head. "Fun idea. But I'm not about to gate-crash some millionaire's fancy drinks party just to spot celebrities."

Claudia sighed. "No, not a good idea, I agree. You can still spot them by sitting at Le Senequier with a drink."

"Le—what?"

"Senequier. It's a famous café on the harbour, downtown. That's where you can sit and see the world go by and spy on the people in the yachts moored by the quayside. A free peep show, if you like that sort of thing. I often sit there and look at them, just for fun, when I've finished for the day."

"I might join you."

"Why not? We might bump into each other some evening. Anyway, it was nice to meet you. I'll be in touch when the dining-room suite is ready to be delivered."

"Okay. I'll open the gate for you."

"Thank you. Have a nice evening. Ciao," Claudia chanted and walked out, leaving a faint whiff of Acqua di Parma behind her.

* * *

A nice evening? What that would that be to Claudia? Not spending it all alone in a huge house, that's for sure. Judging by her good looks and bubbly charm, she probably had a hot boyfriend.

Having walked the dogs in the woods up the hill, this time without meeting anything wild, either boar or Irishman, Daisy had a light dinner of salad and cheese Olivier had left on the terrace, along with a chilled bottle of rosé, before he left. She sat there and watched the sun go down over the headland in the west and wondered what was on the other side. She had seen the name Cap Lardier on the map and knew it was a vast nature reserve and area for walking. Maybe a nice place to walk the dogs sometime.

She took her glass and wandered through the empty house, lingering in the living room, where she sat on one of the sofas for a moment, admiring the now beautiful room and the wonderful paintings. She popped into the dogs' room, hoping they would welcome a cuddle, but they were both fast asleep on their silk cushions. Disappointed that even the dogs didn't want her company, Daisy walked up the stairs and glanced into each of the bedrooms, amazed at the exquisite taste with which they had been decorated.

The last bedroom was the master suite, which Belinda had warned was off limits. But Belinda wasn't around, and Claudia had said it was the most amazing of all the rooms, so it had to be worth a little peep. Emboldened by the wine, Daisy opened the door slowly, her eyes popping at the opulence of the room. She opened the door wider and tiptoed in across the soft white carpet.

The enormous bed was stacked with silk cushions in every colour imaginable. The sofa and chairs were upholstered in striped silk, echoing the theme of the bed. The windows were hung with heavy silk curtains, shimmering in the lamplight, and the antique chest of drawers was crammed with silver ornaments. Daisy opened the door to the bathroom and let out a whistle as she switched on the light. The bathtub by the window was huge, with gold-plated taps in the shape of swans. It was obvious, even in that light, that the views of the garden and the sea were possibly the best in the house from the tub.

Two huge basins stood side by side on the opposite wall, flanked by shelves packed with beauty products for both men and women. His 'n' hers, obviously. Daisy peered at the products. Crème de la Mer, Dior, Yves Saint Laurent. Only the best would have done, probably. No anti-ageing creams, simply hydrating and moisturising products. The woman of the house was obviously not that old. The jars and bottles were unopened, their seals still intact. Ready for use later on, Daisy guessed. On impulse, she dimmed the lights, slid into the tub and peered out at the silent moonlit garden and the sea glinting below. How amazing to lie there in the morning and look at that, and knew you owned it all…

Feeling a bit like Goldilocks, Daisy slowly clambered out of the bathtub, switched off light, and walked out of the bathroom. Time to go to bed. But before that, maybe a peek into one of the wardrobes? She opened the door beside the bathroom and put on the light. A huge walk-in wardrobe with neat rows of clothes, shoes and handbags met her eyes. Whoa, what a fabulous array of designer stuff. Daisy held up a pair of black Louboutins, their trademark red soles glinting. How could anyone possible walk in such high heels? She ran her eyes over the rows of outfits and picked out a deceptively simple, blue, linen, shift dress. Prada, of course. She held it in front of her and studied her reflection in the full-length mirror. Gorgeous. She returned the dress carefully and pulled out a short silk dress by Vera Wang in shimmery turquoise. Wouldn't this be a hit at any party?

Daisy looked at it for a moment and before she could stop herself, stripped out of her shorts and T-shirt and wriggled into the dress. It fitted her perfectly. What a coincidence. The Kedrov woman must also have been a size six. Daisy did a twirl in front of the mirror and admired her reflection. The dress made her look… rich. She pulled back her hair and piled it on top of her head. Lovely. The dress had thin straps holding up the bustier at the front, a fitted waist and a skirt that flared out to just above the knees. The colour enhanced Daisy's brown eyes and turned her hair the colour of dark honey. She took out the Louboutins again and put them on. They were a size too big. What a pity.

After studying herself for a while and imagining going to a party dressed like that, Daisy let out a sigh of regret and took off the dress and the shoes, returning them to where she had found them. She put her own clothes back on and flicked through the other outfits, noting that they were all from top designers, some even from haute-couture houses in Paris. Gee, what a wardrobe. Daisy shook her head in disbelief and returned to the bedroom.

A clicking sound suddenly made her stiffen. What was that? It sounded like—yes, claws on marble. One of the dogs must have decided to join her. She put her glass on the chest of drawers and peered into the corridor. In the dim light, she could see a white fluffy shape coming towards her. Bess.

"Don't let the dogs roam around the house," Belinda had warned. But it was just Bess, a white fluffy ball of cuteness. What harm could she have done? It would be nice to have her company for the night.

Daisy crouched and put out her arms. "Bess, come here. What are you doing out of your room?" Bess whimpered, jumped into Daisy's arms and started to lick her face. Holding the little dog in her arms, Daisy went back into the master suite. She sat on the bed with the dog in her arms, sipping the last of the wine. This was such a fabulous room.

There was an Aladdin's cave aspect about it she liked, something so opulent and ridiculous that was more compelling than the cool elegance of the rest of the house. It was as if the owner's spirit still lingered there. As if they had left a little bit of themselves in the room before they left. It was eerie and strange.

Bess stirred in her arms and snuffled. Then she settled on Daisy's lap and fell asleep. Daisy stroked the soft fur, her thoughts far away. Then she felt something on Bess' collar. A little name tag. Daisy glanced at it and blinked. Then she had a closer look at the dog. This wasn't Bess.

Chapter 5

"Asta," Daisy read aloud from the tag. The dog opened one eye, wagged its little tail, then went back to sleep again. On closer inspection, Daisy realised this dog was not, like Bess, a bichon frisé, but a fox terrier. And it was just a puppy. But how did it get into the house? All the doors were locked and the alarm was on. Maybe it had wandered in during the day or while the furniture was being delivered? Yes, that was it. The little dog had strayed from somewhere, entered the house, gone up the stairs and fallen asleep in one of the bedrooms.

Daisy stroked the soft fur and lifted the flap of an ear, then the other to see if it had a tattoo. But no number marred the soft pink skin inside the ears. She hugged the dog closer.

"You're such a cutie, do you know that? But what the hell am I going to do with you? You can't stay here. The other dogs will probably eat you." She looked down at the warm little bundle on her lap. It must be someone's much-loved new puppy. It probably belonged to a child, who would be desperately trying to find it. Best thing to do was to call the local police station. Belinda had put the number on that list with all the instructions.

With the puppy in her arms, Daisy went to her room, settled the little dog gently on the bed and took out the notebook with the instructions from the small safe. She found the number to the gendarmerie and dialled it.

A sleepy voice replied. "Gendarmerie de Saint-Tropez. Xavier Bernard à votre service."

"Uh, do you speak English?"

"Oui, madame. A leetle bit. Please speak slowly."

"Okay." Daisy cleared her throat and sat down on the bed. "I'm calling about a lost dog. A fox terrier puppy called Asta."

"You lost this dog?"

"No, I found it."

"I don't understand," the officer said, sounding irritated. "If you found it, why are you calling? You lost the dog, then you found it—so?"

"No," Daisy snapped. "Please listen. I found this dog. It's not mine, it belongs to someone else."

"Who?"

"That's what I'm trying to find out."

"Why should we know this? Are you, how do you say, wasting the time of the police?"

Daisy sighed and rolled her eyes. "Nooo. I just thought I'd tell you I'd found this dog and ask if anyone has reported it missing. To the police, I mean."

"Ah. D'accord." Daisy could almost hear the penny drop. "Okay," he continued. "I shall look and see." Daisy could hear a shuffling of papers and some muttering in French: "Chiens perdus…" Then he came back on the line. "Oui, madame, there is a note here. Small white puppy called—"

"Asta?" Daisy whispered.

"Yes."

"Who lost it?"

"It doesn't say."

"But…but there must be an address?"

"Villa Mimosa."

"Where's that?"

"In Saint-Tropez."

"I know," Daisy sighed. "I could figure that out. But where in Saint-Tropez?"

"I can't tell you that. Because of security."

"Oh, shit."

"What?"

"That's merde in your language."

"I know that. But why did you say it?"

"Because I want to know who owns this dog so I can return it to the owner. I can't keep it, even though it's really cute. I'm sure there's a child out there somewhere crying himself to sleep because he's lost his little puppy."

"That's sad." The police officer sounded only slightly more sympathetic.

"Very sad. Oh, come on," Daisy pleaded. "Tell me where the house is so I can give the dog back. I won't tell anyone you told me, I swear."

"You already did."

"What?"

"Swear."

"Oh, crap."

"Now you did it again. That's a rude word in English, n'est-ce pas?"

"You bet." Daisy hovered between the desire to throw the phone across the room and hanging up in his ear.

He heaved an enormous sigh. "All right, madame, this is what we will do—you give me your name and number and I will call the owners and give them the information and then they will call you."

Daisy breathed out slowly. "Finally."

"What?"

"Oh, for Christ's sake. Just listen. My name is Daisy Hennessey…" She spelled her name out slowly. "And I live in Villa—" She stopped. "Never mind. Telling you that might also break the security code."

"You don't trust me?"

"Are you kidding? After this conversation? Anyway," Daisy breezed on, "I'll just give you the number to my cell phone. That's 'portable' in French, by the way."

"I know."

"Gee, I'm impressed. Anyway the number is…" Daisy rattled off the number. "Please tell them they can call me any time."

"Very well, madame. I will do this."

"Thanks a million," Daisy said and hung up. Exhausted, she lay back on the bed, patting the little bundle beside her. She drifted off and slept, fully dressed on top of the bed, with the lights on, until the phone woke her up.

Groggy with sleep, Daisy grabbed her phone. "Hello?"

"Is this Dai-see Enne?" said a female voice. She laughed. "Sorry the policeman didn't seem to be able to pronounce your name." Her voice was warm with just a hint of an Irish accent.

"Daisy Hennessey," Daisy said, suddenly wide awake. "Is this about Asta?"

"Yes. You found her?"

"Yes. Last night. She wandered into my house. I think it must have happened during the afternoon while I was having some furniture delivered. And then I only just found her a couple of hours ago. She's right here, asleep on my bed."

"Thank God! Tommy's been crying his eyes out ever since he let go of the lead and the dog ran off."

"Tommy?"

"That's my nephew. His dad gave him the dog for his birthday. My name's Molly."

"Hi, Molly. Thanks for getting in touch. Tell me where you are and I'll come over with the dog."

"But it's only six thirty in the morning," Molly protested.

"What?" Daisy peered at her watch. "Gee. I slept all night. Seemed only like a minute."

"I'm sorry to have called you so early," Molly said apologetically. "But Tommy woke up and started crying for his dog, so I phoned the police again to see if anyone had found her."

Daisy sat up and yawned. "You mean you had to call them? That nitwit at the station said he'd contact you straight away. That was last night."

"I think they had some sort of emergency after that, he told me. A burglary in one of those fancy villas, so he might have forgotten."

"He seemed like the kind of guy who'd forget his own name. You should have heard our conversation last night. It was like talking to Inspector Clouseau."

Molly giggled. "I know what you mean. Look, I'll tell Tommy Asta's been found and then perhaps I can come and get her?"

"I'll come to you. Much easier. This house is a little bit tricky to find. Where are you?"

"The house is called Villa Mimosa. And it's just off the little beach at the Baie de Canebiers, if you know where that is."

"Yes, I do. I'll be there in about an hour. Is that okay?"

"Perfect. Tommy will be happy. Oh, the house is that ramshackle old wreck at the end of the lane. Looks abandoned, but it's not. Liam just bought it and he's doing it up bit by bit."

"Liam? Your husband?"

"No, my brother."

"Yes, so you said." Daisy laughed. "Nephew—brother, of course. Sorry. My brain isn't working yet. I need coffee and lots of it."

"Me too," Molly said.

Daisy said goodbye and hung up. Asta stirred beside her, stretched and yawned. "You need to pee, I can tell," Daisy said and lifted her up. "I'll sneak down to the little field. Try not to pee on me or anything else in the meantime." She got off the bed, tucked Asta under her arm and made her way downstairs, looking forward to day ahead. It looked very promising.

* * *

With the help of the GPS in the car, Daisy found Villa Mimosa later that morning without too much trouble. She had to laugh as it came into view. Ramshackle was a very apt description. The old villa seemed to sag in the middle and the paint was peeling off the stucco walls. The front garden had been tidied up, but the shrubs and borders needed trimming. The shutters had been repaired and painted green, but some of the windows had broken panes, and the front door didn't close properly. It had a wooden veranda at the front with wonderful views of the bay and the town of Sainte-Maxime on the other side. Here, with the heat reflected by the flat yellow grass, the sound of the crickets was louder than ever.

Daisy parked the car and gently lifted Asta out of the back. The door flew open and a little boy with dark hair burst through the door.

"Asta!" He held out his arms. Daisy let the puppy down. It flew across the yellow grass of the lawn, straight into the arms of the little boy and started to furiously lick his face. The boy collapsed with the puppy still licking him, and the two rolled around on the grass in a heap of fur, barks and giggles.

"Tommy!" A voice shouted from the veranda. "Don't get your clothes all dirty again." A petite woman with red curly hair and what seemed like a million freckles ran down the steps. She stopped when she saw Daisy. "Hi. You must be Daisy." She held out her hand. "I'm Molly."

"From Ireland, right?" Daisy said as she shook Molly's hand. On closer inspection she guessed Molly to be in her late thirties. Her handshake was firm and her eyes friendly. A very attractive woman in a bohemian sort of way, with her peasant skirt, several rows of wooden beads and that wild, curly, red hair. She exuded a warmth that made Daisy like her instantly.

"Ha, ha, how did you guess?" Molly laughed, her blue eyes twinkling.

"I don't know," Daisy said. "The accent and the red hair, maybe? Or those blue eyes? Only Irish people have eyes that blue."

"You seem to know a lot about Ireland."

"My dad was Irish. I'm from New York myself. I've been to Dublin a few times. But my mom was Italian. I'm a bit of a mongrel, really."

"They're the best," Molly laughed. "Thanks for bringing Asta back. Tommy's been miserable since she ran off."

"I'm happy I could get her safely back home. Even if I wouldn't have minded keeping her. She's so cute."

Molly nodded. "Yes, but she's a bit of handful right now. Chewing on everything and not quite house-trained yet. Drives Liam nuts."

"Liam? Your brother?"

"Yes, that's right. Tommy's dad. He's a writer. You might have heard of him. Liam Creedon?"

Daisy wracked her brain. Then it came to her. "Oh, yes. He wrote those popular political thrillers set in Cork, right? I haven't read any of them, but I've seen them on the best-seller lists."

"That's right," Molly said. "He wrote the first one when he was only twenty-five. And he's still writing them. He's working on a screenplay right now. That's why he needed me to spend the summer here to help out with Tommy."

I looked up at the house. "He's here?"

"Yes. And up already, writing. There's a lot of pressure on him at the moment after his latest book was made into a movie and won an Oscar for best screenplay. Not easy, as he gets invited everywhere, too, being a celebrity and all, which he hates. But he has to go out there and be seen and meet people, his agent says, so he does his best."

"Oh," was all Daisy managed.

The front door opened suddenly, and a man dressed in nothing but pyjama pants stepped out on the veranda. "Molly? What's all this noise?"

Daisy blinked and stared at the man in shock. It was him. No mistaking the black hair, the rough, handsome features and that voice. The man with the shotgun up in the woods. He looked even more dishevelled than before with his unshaven face, messy hair and the pyjama pants hanging off his slim hips. His torso was trim and tanned and his eyes the blazing blue she had noticed in the woods. They focused on Daisy.

"Bloody hell, if it isn't the dog lady."

"Holy crap," she stammered. "What are you doing here? I mean, of course, it's you and you must be…Liam Creedon."

He frowned and hitched up the pyjama pants. "Guilty. But I don't know who the hell you are, do I? Except that you're an American who lives in one of those millionaire villas."

"Dad!" Tommy shouted and scrambled to his feet with a wriggling Asta in his arms. "Asta came back! She ran away and you said we'd never see her again, but here she is. And that lady brought her back."

Liam's face softened, and he went down the steps to the lawn, ruffled Tommy's hair and gave Asta a pat. "That's great news, Tommy. Really great. I was getting a bit sad meself listenin' to your cryin'."

Daisy noticed how soft Liam's Cork accent was when he spoke to his son. But when he looked at her, his expression changed.

Daisy took a step back. "Well, I…um…had better be going. I have to have breakfast and walk the dogs and—"

Molly turned to her. "Why don't you have breakfast here? I've just made some scones and I'll make a pot of tea. What do you say, Liam?"

"Yeah, sure, why not? I might even get dressed to honour the occasion," Liam added, but he didn't look as if he was delighted at the prospect.

"No. I'll have to be going," Daisy said with regret. Despite Liam's obvious hostility, it would have been such a treat to sit on the veranda and have breakfast with this unusual family. But she had to get back to her duties and the dogs, the house and—the solitude.

"Ah, we're not fancy enough, are we?" Liam teased. "I'm sure you live in some luxury pad, judging by that car."

"I...well, I do, but it's not my fault," Daisy blurted out.

Liam winked. "Tough, but someone's got to do it, you mean?"

"Liam!" Molly chided. "Why are you being so rude?" She turned to Daisy. "He's a bit of a grump in the morning."

"Ah, sure, I was only teasing her." Liam grinned and scratched his head. "But in any case, I have to get back to my work. Someone's just found a headless body. Gotta sort that out and it's only the first draft."

Daisy nodded. "Me too. No headless body but a lot of barking dogs."

"Tommy, say thank you to Daisy for bringing Asta back," Molly ordered.

Tommy turned his cute freckly face to Daisy and looked at her over Asta's soft fur. "Thanks for bringing my dog back. Will you come back and play with us?"

"Yes, I will," Daisy said and put her arm around Tommy, giving him a little squeeze. "You bet. Very soon."

"You can come to my birthday party. I'll be six." Tommy said. "It's next week. How old are you?"

"Thirty-two," Daisy said without thinking.

"Is that old?" Tommy wanted to know.

"Very old." Daisy winked at him.

"My dad's older than you. He's forty-one. And Auntie Molly is thirty-eight, and that's really old, but I'm not allowed to tell anyone."

Daisy laughed. "You just told me."

Tommy's face fell. "I couldn't help it. I'm sorry, Auntie Moll."

"It's okay," Daisy soothed. "The secret's safe with me. I won't tell anyone, even if they roast me over a fire."

Tommy looked at her suspiciously, and then his face broke into a gap-toothed grin. "Nah, that won't happen."

"I hope not. But in any case, I forgot what you just said. How old is your Auntie Molly again?"

Tommy laughed. "You're funny. Oh, please come to my party, will ya?"

Daisy glanced at Liam Creedon. "Thanks, but I think it'll be better if you ask someone your own age."

"I already did," Tommy said. "All the boys from the kid's beach camp are coming."

"That's great," Daisy said. "Then you don't need old people like me."

"We have enough oldies with Molly and me." Liam walked back up the steps to the veranda. "Got to get back to work. Just came to see what all the noise was about. Could you keep it down from now on, please?"

"Terribly sorry," Daisy snapped. "I'm sure the noise of a happy little boy was extremely annoying. You could at least say thank you."

Liam stopped and threw her a glance over his shoulder. "Yeah, thanks for bringing the mutt back."

"You're welcome," Daisy said, but the door had already banged shut behind him. She felt like sticking her tongue out but stopped herself in time. What would Molly have thought? "What's with the clay-pigeon shooting?" she asked instead.

"Oh that." Molly sighed. "He does that to get rid of his anger and frustration. He's had a lot of problems he finds hard to deal with. Demons, you know?" She glanced at Tommy, and put her finger to her mouth. "Some other time," she murmured.

"Of course." Daisy looked up at the house again and could see Liam's figure moving in an upstairs room. He saw her and pulled the curtains shut. "Well, bye for now," she said to Molly.

"See you soon," Molly said. "Please call again. We'd love to have you. Liam too, even if he doesn't show it."

"I wouldn't be too sure about that," Daisy said, remembering Liam's angry stare at her. "He seems to hate me. Or is it women in general?"

Molly nodded. "Something like that. Long story."

"Then we have something in common. I'm not too fond of men at the moment. Especially the angry kind. That's another long story." Daisy started to walk away, feeling she had said too much.

"Stories," Molly said. "Don't we all have them?"

Chapter 6

The rest of the week was uneventful, one day following the next in much the same fashion. Daisy walked the dogs in a different part of the woods, closer to the main road, where there was less risk of any wild animals or bumping into Liam Creedon. When she came back, she went for a swim in the pool and then had a late breakfast on the terrace, served by a silent Olivier. Daisy sometimes tried to strike up a conversation but gave up when she only got monosyllabic replies. He obviously felt he had already told her too much about himself. The rest of the day was taken up with more dog duties, a swim off the beach, dinner and a movie picked out from the huge DVD collection in the library. She didn't follow orders to the letter and let the dogs out to join her in the den when she was watching movies. She liked having them around. Ivan seemed happy to snooze on the rug, and Bess usually cuddled up with her on the sofa. She found them surprisingly good company, especially Bess.

Daisy had swung past Villa Mimosa twice on her way home from her walks, hoping to see Molly and Tommy. On both occasions the front garden was deserted and all the shutters closed. They must have either been away or out for the day. Perhaps it wasn't such a good idea to call on them at all. Liam Creedon had been positively hostile when Daisy took Tommy's dog back.

At the end of the first week, cabin fever started to set

in. Late one morning, when Olivier had cleared away the breakfast dishes, Daisy stayed on the terrace, sipping the last of her coffee, staring out over the vast expanse of lawns and sea. The sky was as blue as ever, the sun as hot and the crickets as loud. The sea was dotted with little sails, and she could see a lone windsurfer setting out from the shore. A light breeze ruffled Daisy's hair and cooled her hot face. She sighed. It was a heavenly place for a holiday or even for living there permanently—but barren and sad without company. The much-longed-for solitude now looked increasingly terrifying. A few days on her own had been good, but six weeks? Even though the encounter with Molly, Tommy and even Liam was a huge relief, it wouldn't have been possible to call on them that often. And it wouldn't have been a good idea to get too close. Daisy decided to give Flora a call. She was probably a little lonely, too, stuck in the house, waiting for the birth of her child.

Flora answered on the first ring. "Hello, oui? Flora Belcourt."

"You're getting awfully French," Daisy teased.

"Daisy!" Flora squealed. "Where are you? Where did you disappear to? We were all so worried about you. And Ross is behaving as if you'd *died*."

"Ross?" Daisy paused. "Please don't tell him I called. I mean, you can just let him know I'm all right, but don't tell him where I am. Don't tell *anyone*, okay?"

"How can I? I don't *know* where you are."

"Oh. Yes. Of course. You don't."

"Are you going to tell me?"

"No, yes, well…" Daisy thought for a moment. It wouldn't have done any harm to tell Flora. She could keep a secret. "I'm not that far away. Look, I'm not going to tell you exactly where I am because it would make it awkward for you. If you don't know, you can't tell."

"Yes, you're right. Okay. Anyway, I've other things on my mind right now."

"Of course. Gee, you must think I'm very selfish. How are you? Has that baby come out yet? How's little Kieran?"

"I'm fine. The baby's due any day now. Might even be today, the way I'm feeling. My sister-in-law took Kieran for a couple of days to let me rest. Toddlers sure are exhausting. And Philippe's working in his studio, doing a shoot for an ad. He's not leaving my side for a moment, he says. So that's how I am. Big as a house, of course. Backache, heartburn. The usual."

"You don't fool me. You're blissfully happy."

"Of course. I'm ecstatic. Anyway," Flora sighed. "Go on, mystery woman. Tell me what you're doing."

"I have a job. It's a weird job in a weird place and I'm beginning to regret taking it. I mean," Daisy continued, gazing out over the pool, "it's a heavenly place. Totally surreal. But kind of sterile. Like being stranded on a planet or something. Planet Rich."

"What's your job, then?"

"Dog-sitting. And sitting the house too. It's huge and luxurious with incredible bedrooms and bathrooms, an infinity pool and a private beach and a butler who serves me delicious food and wine and—"

"And—?"

"I hate it," Daisy said and burst into tears.

"What? Hold on a minute, I have to get comfortable." Flora seemed to shuffle around for a bit and then came back. "Okay. I've put my feet up and got myself some iced tea. I'm listening.

Daisy sniffled. "I don't want to bother you with my problems."

"It's okay. I was getting bored resting, anyway. Come on, tell me. First of all, why did you run away from Ross? I know you didn't want him to get any ideas, but wouldn't it have been better to tell him? I mean, he's mad about you but he would have accepted it."

"I know. But running to his house when I broke up with Bruno was a huge mistake. Not fair to Ross. I was such a mess and then he was so nice and—" Daisy stopped and dabbed her eyes with the linen napkin beside her cup. "I didn't want to see the hurt in his eyes when I told him. So I ran."

"I see. Not very brave of you, of course. But maybe you don't want to hear that right now?"

"No. It's no use. *I'm* no use."

"What's this all about?" Flora asked. "Some kind of self-flagellation? So you're not physically attracted to Ross. No big deal. It's all about chemistry, isn't it?"

"I must be mad," Daisy sighed. "He's so perfect in every way."

Flora let out a laugh. "And that's why you don't fancy him. You like a man with flaws and a bad attitude."

"Then I try to tame him but it never works. Guys like that can't be tamed."

"You might find one who can be one day."

"Fat chance," Daisy sighed, the face of Liam Creedon fleeting through her mind. But he was completely out of her league. She could never have tamed a wild Irishman.

Chapter 7

While she was having coffee on the terrace after her morning walk with the dogs, Daisy reflected on how different Saint-Tropez and its surroundings were from the area around Nice and Cannes. Here, the vineyards dominated the landscape, and it was more rural than around the more fashionable towns. Saint-Tropez itself, although always 'in', had never lost its old-world Provençal atmosphere. The glitz and glamour were grafted onto an old and beautiful culture, where art, literature and music thrived. You didn't have to look rich there; in fact, it wasn't accepted. The casual, quiet elegance of old money ruled. That was the entrance card to the inner sanctum of high society of Saint-Tropez. The newly rich were accepted on sufferance but always considered as the necessary evil.

Chantal told Daisy all about it once, when they had gone there to look at a house they were planning put on their books. Gabriel, Chantal's partner, was of that old Saint-Tropez aristocracy and a renowned artist in his own right. You couldn't buy yourself in, Chantal explained; you were either born or married into it. There were two societies: old money and new. Old money was probably boring, while the nouveau-riche people seemed to have a lot more fun. What was the use of having lots of money if you didn't spend it?

Daisy changed into her swimsuit and jumped into the pool. Swimming had always been her favourite sport, and in the huge pool, she could do a real workout. She did fifty laps before she stopped, the exercise having improved her mood. She came to the conclusion that leaving what happened behind and looking forward were the best things to do.

She got out of the pool and dried herself on the fluffy white towel Olivier had placed on the lounger. Always a step ahead, always knowing what she wanted seconds before she knew it herself. The man had to be psychic. She looked around, hoping to catch him and say thank you, but he had slipped away.

As she got dressed, Daisy could hear church bells in the distance. Sunday mass in Saint-Tropez. She hadn't been to mass for years, despite her Catholic upbringing. Not quite sure what she actually believed, she had become a lapsed Catholic and only went to church for weddings and the odd funeral. But the sound of bells in the still air was oddly compelling. Why not go and just listen to the hymns in that beautiful old church and then go to the Sunday market afterwards? She nodded to herself. Good idea. Best idea for a long time, actually. She mentally patted herself on the back, looking forward to the day ahead. After locking up the dogs securely, she got her handbag, slipped out through the gate and walked down the alleyway towards the centre of town and the church.

* * *

The church of Notre-Dame de l'Assomption, situated in the centre of the old town of Saint-Tropez, was easy to find. Its yellow clock tower and terracotta façade rose above the old buildings, standing out against the intense blue of the Mediterranean. Inside the cool interior, Daisy squeezed into a space in a pew between two old ladies dressed in black. During the many long readings in French, Daisy's eyes wandered, taking in the beautiful baroque decorations, the religious paintings and the statue of Saint-Tropez, the patron saint of the town.

As the mass continued, the smell of incense, the singing and murmured prayers of the congregation took Daisy back to her childhood and her many summer holidays in Ireland. Going to mass with Granny and then buying the Sunday papers, Dad going to the pub with 'the lads' and the women and children returning home to make lunch. Later on, the Sunday papers were read beside the fire, and then they all went for a long walk in the Dublin Mountains. Daisy blinked back tears and said a little prayer for both her granny and her dad. They were together in heaven now, her mother had said. A comforting thought, whether it was true or not, but at the age of twelve, Daisy had believed it. She still did.

The mass ended and Daisy rose to file out of the church with the rest of the congregation, not forgetting to bless herself with holy water from the font by the door. The parish priest greeted everyone outside. Blinded by the bright sunshine and slightly dazed after the long mass, Daisy shook his warm hand and smiled, unable to find the words in French. But the priest, a stocky man with grey hair and twinkly blue eyes, didn't let go of her hand.

"Hello," he said in English. "Are you here on holiday?"

Daisy couldn't help smiling back. "No. I work here in Saint-Tropez. I'm from America."

He patted her hand. "Excellent. I hope you'll be happy here in our town."

"Thank you. I'm sure I will."

He smiled, let go of her hand and turned to the next person in line. Wobbling in her high heels on the cobblestones, Daisy walked through the maze of alleys until she came to the Place des Lices and the Sunday market.

The big square was packed with stalls, selling everything from fruit, vegetables, cheese, olive oil and wine to clothes,

shoes and household equipment. The warm air was perme-
ated with smells from the food stalls and garlic, herbs, olive
oil and spices all mingled into a heady mix of what Daisy
always thought of as the perfume of Provençe. If you could
bottle it, you could make a fortune.

Wandering from stall to stall, Daisy sampled olives, pieces
of bread, strawberries, bits of exotic fruit, ham, cheese, pâté,
and the odd slurp of wine the stallholders pressed upon her.
At the far end of the square, where clothes, shoes, ceramics
and small artefacts were laid out, Daisy saw a familiar figure.
She came to an abrupt stop in front of a display of beautifully crafted handmade jewellery and stared at the woman
behind it.

"Molly!"

She looked up. "Hello, Daisy." With her wild red curls,
beads and bangles, and dressed in a white peasant smock
and wide, red, linen pants, Molly blended perfectly with the
other artists selling their wares in this part of the market.

"I didn't know you designed jewellery."

Molly laughed. "You didn't ask. But yes, this is what I do."

Daisy glanced at the bracelets, earrings and necklaces
laid out on blue velvet. They were simple and stunning, con-
sisting mostly of semi-precious stones set in beaten silver.
She picked up a necklace with large aquamarines.

"This one is gorgeous. Can I try it on?"

"Of course. I'll help you with the clasp."

When Daisy had put on the necklace, Molly held up a
mirror for her to see how it looked. It was beautiful. The
large stones lay against Daisy's chest, enhancing her smooth
skin and golden tan.

"It's beautiful," she murmured, watching the stones
twinkle in the sunlight. "I don't think I've ever worn anything this stunning."

"It really suits you," Molly said.

"How much is it?"

"A hundred and fifty euros." Molly hesitated. "But you can have it for ninety. I always give friends a discount."

"Oh, but…" Daisy fingered the necklace. It seemed to belong there, sitting perfectly just above the neckline of her white linen top. She nodded and delved into her bag. "I have to have it. Thank you, Molly." She fished some euro notes out of her wallet. "I don't have much cash on me, but I think there's enough here." Daisy handed Molly the notes, wondering what she would have said if she knew it was nearly all she had until she got paid at the end of the month.

Molly counted the money and put it in her wallet. "Yes, it's all there. Perfect. Here, take it off and I'll put it in a box for you."

Daisy took off the necklace, feeling oddly naked without it and handed it to Molly, who put it in a small wooden box, which she wrapped in lavender tissue paper.

"Do you come here every Sunday?" Daisy asked.

"Only when I have something to sell. It takes a little while to make these. I also sell online from my website."

Daisy looked at the other pieces, all beautiful in their simple design. "I love them all. They look really expensive. I bet you'd sell for a lot more if you tried one of the fancy shops down by the harbour, where all the yachts are moored."

"I'm sure I would. But I prefer to be my own boss. If I sold through those shops, I'd have to give them a huge discount and also have to produce a lot more." Molly laughed. "Freedom is worth more than money."

"That's true."

Molly looked at her watch. "The market's nearly over. Why don't we go down to the Senequier and grab a coffee? My treat."

Daisy put the box in her bag. "Sounds lovely. I'll just have time before I have to walk the dogs. But it's only a short walk to the house from here, so there's no panic."

"Great. If you help me pack up, we can be on our way a

lot quicker. Liam's coming to take the pieces home and put them in the safe. I think he'll be here in just a minute."

"Liam?" Daisy said. The pleasure of bumping into Molly waned. "Is he bringing Tommy?"

Molly started to put the pieces of jewellery into boxes. "No, Tommy had a play date with a little English boy. Thank goodness he's made some friends at last. He was getting very lonely."

Daisy carefully placed earrings and bracelets into little velvet pockets, which she transferred to the box Molly handed her.

"What about his mother?" she asked casually.

Molly sighed. "His mum died when he was only two. So Liam's all alone with his little boy. Not easy. Especially for someone like Liam."

"Why especially for someone like—" Daisy stopped abruptly as Liam suddenly appeared at the stand.

He looked startled to see her there. "Well, well, look who's here," he drawled.

Daisy felt her face flush. "Hi," she mumbled while she put the last of the pieces away. "I'm giving Molly a hand."

"How very gracious of you," he said. "Good deed of the day, is it?"

Daisy stiffened. "May I ask what the hell you mean by that? What's your problem?"

"Yes," Molly cut in. "Liam, why are you so rude to Daisy? First, when she brought Asta back and just now."

Liam smiled and shook his head "Ah, come on, I'm teasing. Can't you see that? Or are you the thin-skinned kind?"

"Not normally, no," Daisy replied. "But it wasn't obvious to me that you were only joking. Nobody laughed."

Liam held out his hand. "Okay, I'm sorry. Perhaps I was a little rude. Let's shake hands and be friends."

Daisy put her hand in his and looked into his bright-blue

eyes that twinkled with mischief mingled with something else that was barely discernible. Bitterness? Or something akin to anger and rage. A man with a lot of baggage. Not someone to get involved with.

"Of course," she said, keeping her voice cool, pulling her hand away after the brief touch. "No hard feelings. A little teasing never hurt anyone, right?"

"Right," Liam said, and turned to Molly. "Did you sell much today?"

"Two pairs of earrings. You know, the turquoise ones set in silver. Then three bracelets and three necklaces, apart from the one Daisy just bought."

Liam looked at Daisy. "You bought a necklace from Molly?"

"Yes," Daisy replied. "Why are you so surprised? It's a beautiful necklace. In fact, all the pieces here are exquisite."

Liam's expression softened. "I'd accuse you of charity if I didn't agree. My sister's work is exceptional. Molly, if you have everything packed up, we can go home."

"No, I'm having a coffee with Daisy at the harbour. Then I'm going to do a bit of shopping and have lunch before I go home."

Liam shrugged. "Grand. I'll collect Tommy, then." He threw a look over his shoulder at Daisy as he walked off. "Bye, princess."

Daisy was about to respond with a bitchy remark, but he left as suddenly as he had arrived. She could see him further up the street, loading Molly's boxes into his Ferrari. He got into the car and drove off in a shower of dust.

"A complicated man," she said more to herself than to Molly.

Molly glanced at the car driving off. "That's putting it mildly. Let's forget about him and have that coffee. My treat."

They walked the short distance to the harbour, where a row of gleaming white yachts were moored at the crowded quayside. The Senequier with its red awning was just across the pavement, and Molly and Daisy soon found a table in the front row, where they could watch the world go by while enjoying a very expensive cup of espresso.

"Worth it for the floorshow, though," Molly said and picked up her cup.

"Absolutely." Daisy tried not to stare at one celebrity after the other filing past. "Was that Joan Collins?" she asked, eyeing the back of an elegant elderly brunette on the arm of a much younger man.

Molly followed her gaze. "Yes. She has a house up in the hills somewhere. She often comes downtown to shop. Lovely woman, don't you think?"

"Amazing." Daisy lifted her cup but hiccupped as George Clooney and his wife walked past. "Oh my God, it's *them*," she whispered.

"Who?" Molly asked whipping around.

"George Clooney and his new wife. Look they're getting into that white Mercedes over there. I bet they're staying at some fancy villa somewhere."

"Shit, I missed them. I was looking at the king of Sweden. He has a house just across the bay." Molly pointed towards Sainte-Maxime. "There. The one with the blue shutters."

Daisy looked across the bay, where a white villa with blue shutters was clearly visible.

"Yes, I know," she said trying to look as if she was used to royalty and celebrity. But she sighed inwardly. Lucky them to have their own house there. How fantastic it would be to come and go as you please and have enough money to do anything or buy anything you wanted. Daisy studied Molly. "You look all dreamy-eyed. Being wealthy and famous isn't all it's cracked up to be," she said with studied nonchalance. "Great to have all that money, yes. But to be a celebrity and always have to dodge the press? I'm glad I'm not famous."

"Oh, but the clothes and shoes," Molly sighed. "And

dressing up and going to parties. The glamour, the buzz... being rich has always been my favourite daydream."

"Why?" Daisy asked. "Money doesn't buy happiness."

"Maybe not," Molly said. "But if you're miserable anyway, it's nicer in comfort."

"That's true. I'm glad I don't have to scratch for a living as well as—"

"Being miserable?" Molly asked. "Are you?"

Daisy shrugged. "Sort of. Usual story. I fall for the wrong men all the time, and then I end up miserable at regular intervals. It's happened again just recently. Sexy guy who turned out to be a real jerk. I never learn, that's my problem. Then there was this other guy who seemed perfect, but I just couldn't fall in love with him."

"He was rich?"

Daisy nodded. "Yeah, but that's beside the point. I just wasn't attracted to him in a physical way, if you know what I mean. No chemistry or the wrong chemistry, anyway."

"You're lucky. You never have the dilemma of being tempted by money," Molly said wistfully. "But some women wouldn't hesitate."

"I would never be with someone for money," Daisy declared. "Even if I were broke. Would you?"

Molly burst out laughing. "Are you kidding? Of course I would. If the man wasn't half bad, I'd be quite happy to say 'I do'. Lots of money can turn the plainest man into a handsome hunk."

Daisy stared at Molly. "Are you serious?"

"Absolutely. Why not?" Molly laughed. "I'd put up with a lot of misery for a bit of cash. Even bad sex."

"Really? Would you?"

"Of course. Don't sit there looking all precious. It goes on here, there and everywhere. Especially here." Molly made a sweep of her arm toward the yachts. "Just look at those floating plastic palaces and those gorgeous women sitting on deck. Don't pretend you don't know how most of them got there. Nothing to do with true love."

Daisy had to laugh. "Yeah, okay. You're right."

Molly peered at Daisy over the rim of her cup. "That's a relief. I was worried there for a moment. Thought you might be too goody-two-shoes to be true."

"Not at all. I'm a realist and I know what goes on."

"But you don't have to put up with it, being wealthy yourself. Perhaps that's why you can indulge in feelings and true love."

"I suppose." Daisy paused. "Still, I can't help feeling bad about—"

"That nice guy you didn't fancy?" Molly filled in.

"Something like that. I'm so fond of him but—"

"So? What happened?"

"Nothing much. We were friends but he wanted more."

"A misunderstanding, was it? He thought you felt like him but you didn't?"

"Yes. And then I ended up hurting him, which I hated." Suddenly unable to go on, Daisy looked into her empty cup. "Sorry. I shouldn't have mentioned it. I don't really want to talk about it."

Molly nodded and patted Daisy's arm. "I'll listen whenever you need to talk." She pushed away her cup and stood up. "But I have to go if I'm to do any shopping. Tommy will want his lunch and a nap when he comes home. I like to keep him out of the midday sun. Too hot for small children. I'm going to take him to Ireland soon. We've been invited to stay with a friend who has a farm near Clonakilty. We'll be there for two weeks. Tommy will love that." Molly beamed a brilliant smile at Daisy. "I'll call you when I get back. I'm so glad I met you, Daisy. I have no real friends here. But now, I feel as if I have at least one."

Daisy smiled back at Molly. "Me too. I have a feeling we could have a lot of fun. Thanks for coffee. I'll stay here for a bit and then I have to go and take care of my pooches. Have fun in Ireland."

"Thanks. I'm sure I will. Bye, Daisy. Take care."

After Molly had left, Daisy sat at the café, staring out across the bay, wondering how on earth she had landed in this situation: lying to people, pretending she was rich. All because she was bored and needed some excitement. She had to come clean. Tell Molly, who was such a sweetie, the truth. She nodded to herself. Yes, she would. Soon.

Chapter 8

A week later, the cabin fever got a lot worse. With Molly gone and no sign of the lovely Claudia, Daisy was all alone with nobody to talk to. While she managed to keep busy during the day, the evenings yawned ahead with nothing to do. The movies in the library soon lost their appeal, and as Daisy hated anything to do with Facebook or any other social media on the Internet, she found herself wandering idly through the house or sitting on the terrace staring morosely out to sea, thinking she had to find something to do or she would go mad. But what?

She could hear music and laughter from the gardens of the villas nearby. Parties and dinners. How fabulous it would be to dress up and go out to something like that—to drink champagne and flirt and chat with all kinds of people. Had she been married to the owner of this house, she would have been at those parties, judging by the invitations that arrived in the post at regular intervals. She would have just slipped into one of those designer dresses and gone. Then a thought struck her. Why not? The invitations were there and so were the clothes, all hanging in a row in that walk-in wardrobe. All she had to do was to slip into one of them, grab an invitation and...no. She shook her head. That was crazy. But the devil on her shoulder whispered: *Yes, why not? What have you got to lose? What about that invitation for the party tonight you forgot to reply to?*

Daisy went to the office and picked up the most recent invitation card. The party was later that evening, at a villa called La Farniente, which she knew was Italian for 'do nothing'. She had meant to reply to it and wondered if it was too late. Then she saw the tiny writing under the R.S.V.P.: *Regrets only*. Perfect. As she hadn't replied, the hosts, whoever Mr. and Mrs. Schlossenburgh were, would still think the Kedrovs would be going. Or just one of them. She looked at herself in the hall mirror.

"Daisy Kedrov, I presume?" she simpered and then shook her head.

No, she couldn't pretend to be one of them, as she hadn't a clue who they were or even which country they came from. Better to be Daisy Hennessy, their American cousin. She thought for a moment. Of course! She nodded to herself and smiled.

"My mother was of the American branch of the Kedrovs and married a Hennessey," she drawled. Not exactly a lie and if she acted her part, everyone would assume...she laughed to herself as she went to the master bedroom and the walk-in wardrobe, where she flicked through the clothes on the rail. What would be the right thing to wear?

Daisy quickly found the turquoise silk Vera Wang dress she had tried on. It would be perfect, teamed with her own white, strappy, high-heeled sandals, as she didn't have the nerve to walk around in those six-inch heels. She took the dress to her bedroom, slipped it on and applied make-up—not too much, just enough to enhance her tan and bring out her eyes. Her hair, expertly cut into by her hairdresser in Antibes, gave her that well-groomed classy look she was aiming for. As she admired herself in the wall mirror, she realised Molly's necklace would go well with the turquoise silk. She put it on and nearly gasped at how lovely it looked; it followed the neckline of the dress as if it had been made for it.

"Oh, wow," she said as she twirled in front of the mirror. "You look stunning, darling."

Her eyes sparkled as she thought of the adventure ahead, not feeling the slightest bit nervous.

"You *will* go to the ball, Cinderella," she said to her image in the mirror. "And you don't even have to run off at midnight." A few light dabs of Opium on her pulse points, and she was ready to go to.

* * *

Villa Farniente was only a short walk up the hill. Once at the gates, Daisy showed her invitation to a uniformed security guard, who checked it against a list of names.

"Kedrov?" he said.

Daisy nodded, her hands clammy. Of course. They would check the names. "That's right."

"Okay." He took her card and clicked a remote control to open the iron gates. Daisy slipped inside as soon as she could before he asked any more questions. She had to pretend to be a Kedrov or risk getting arrested. She didn't fancy facing that stupid police officer or any of his colleagues. They probably didn't have much of a sense of humour. Pushing away such thoughts, she started up the wide steps to the entrance door that loomed above. She heard laughter and music and the popping of champagne corks as she reached the top of the steps. The double doors were open, and Daisy followed the noise, walking across marble floors through a vast drawing room, furnished nearly entirely in white, until she came to French windows opening onto a wide terrace, where a large group of elegant people were drinking champagne and chatting to each other around the pool.

A tall balding man with kind eyes and a warm smile, dressed in a white tuxedo, walked up to her.

"Hello and welcome." He held out his hand. "I'm Klaus Schlossenburgh. Who are you?"

Shit, the host. Would he spot her as an intruder? Daisy returned his smile and batted her eyelashes.

"Hi, I'm Daisy," she said and shook his hand.

"Daisy—?" he said looking slightly confused.

"Just Daisy," she laughed. "Nobody ever calls me anything else

He nodded. "Aha. That's your professional name, then? You're a model?"

"Not exactly. But yes, I'm in the— fashion business."

"I see. Like Marianne, my wife." He nodded at a tall stunning woman in a white dress, her mane of light-blonde hair tumbling down her back. "I'm sure she'll be happy to see you. Why don't you go and say hello and I'll get someone to bring you some champagne?"

"Okay," Daisy said. "Thanks." When the host walked off, she hesitated, not quite sure what to do. But the hostess had spotted her. Excusing herself to the group, she glided across the terrace, holding out her hand.

"Hello and welcome."

Daisy shook the woman's slim hand. "Hi, Marianne. Nice to see you again," she gushed.

"Uh, yes. Lovely. Where did we meet?" Marianne laughed. "I meet so many people, it's hard to remember everyone." She spoke with a slight Scandinavian accent that added extra charm to her slightly husky voice. Her huge sapphire-blue eyes added a Madonna-like quality to her perfect features. "Was it at the beach club?"

"I can't remember." Daisy chortled. "Must have been in Cannes, I think."

"At the film festival? Were you there, too?"

Daisy nodded. "Yes, I was," she said, which wasn't a lie, as she had been in the crowd outside the festival palace for hours, ogling the stars on the red carpet. "Great festival."

"Wonderful. Klaus was one of the backers for the Johnny Depp movie. You know, the thriller based on the book by that Irish crime writer. What's his name again?"

"Liam Creedon?" Daisy felt an odd sensation as she said his name.

"Yes, that's him. I even think we invited him tonight. Have you seen him?"

"Uh, no." Daisy looked around nervously. Was Liam there? She didn't fancy bumping into him. "I don't really know him, to be honest."

Marianne let out a giggle. "Neither do I. Someone said he's a real hunk but such a recluse. Very difficult to get him to come to parties."

"Yes, so I've heard."

"If you see him, give me a whistle. I really want to talk to him. I love his books. Have you read them?"

"No. But I think there are some in the library of my house," Daisy replied. "Must look them up."

"I can recommend them," Marianne said. "If you can't find any, let me know. I have his whole collection here…if you like reading, of course."

"Love it. I'm reading a Scandinavian crime series at the moment. Stieg Larsson. I'm sure you've read them too."

Marianne nodded with delight in her eyes. "Of course. Fantastic series. I love books." She leaned closer to Daisy. "Not many of the women here do. Possibly because they can't read."

Daisy let out a giggle as she glanced at a busty brunette falling out of tight, silver, lamé dress. "I think I see what you mean," she muttered back.

"Marianne," a man called from the other side of the terrace. "Come over here so we can meet your friend."

Marianne took Daisy by the elbow. "Come and say hello to some great people. They're all in the film and TV business. Much more fun than stupid models." She peered at Daisy. "You're not a model, are you?"

"No," Daisy laughed. "Absolutely not."

"Good. I did some modelling before I married Klaus. He rescued me from that world. Awful bitches, every one of them."

"Must be a very harsh world all right." Daisy took a glass of champagne from the tray of a passing waiter and followed Marianne to the group, where she was introduced to a number of glamorous people with very strange names.

"Are you an actress?" a bald deeply tanned man asked her.

"No, uh, well…I'm resting at the moment," Daisy said.

He nodded. "Me too. It's tough, isn't it? Haven't had as much as a walk-on part since my last job six months ago. But the money was good, so I'll survive. Who's your agent?"

"I'm between agents right now," Daisy said, wondering how she could get away. "I'm thinking of getting into something else, actually. More in the production and stage-setting," she babbled on, feeling like she was about to drown in a sea of fibs. "Or costumes." She drained her glass, which a waiter topped up immediately.

"Love your necklace," a woman in a black dress said. "Who is it by?"

"By?" Daisy asked. "Oh, who made it, you mean?"

She nodded. "Yes. Looks like Chanel, except it's too rough. Must be something American. Am I right?"

Daisy touched the stones. "It's by…Molly. The…the New York designer. Just launched her new collection. Have you heard of her?"

The woman looked impressed. "I think so. In any case, it's fabulous. Does she sell in Europe?"

"No. Not yet," Daisy said. "But she will. Soon."

"You must let me know." The woman fished a card out of her Chanel evening bag. Here are my details. E-mail me as soon as you know when Molly's new boutique is open. Is she planning on Paris or London?"

Daisy blinked. "Both, I think," she said taking the card. "But you can also buy some of her pieces online." She tried desperately to remember if Molly had mentioned a website address.

"Online?" the woman said. "Not a good idea. Then you can't try anything on. Must go. We're going on to the Byblos. Don't forget to contact me." She waved her hand as if she were royalty and disappeared into the crowd.

More guests arrived as the sun set and the sky darkened. The lights on the terrace came on as if by magic. The champagne flowed and delicious canapés were served on large platters. Daisy found herself chatting easily with everyone, making up stories as she went, drinking rather a lot of champagne. She was amazed that nobody seemed to question her presence, despite having never seen her before. Even though the women eyed her with certain suspicion, the men were charming and openly flirtatious, and she basked in their admiration. It made her feel popular and wanted as if she had suddenly come alive after a long, deep sleep.

She was talking to a handsome Italian with the longest eyelashes she had ever seen on a man, when she spotted him. Liam Creedon, just arrived, being greeted by the hostess. Daisy moved so the back of the Italian shielded her from view and peered at Liam while her companion droned on about his yacht. Liam was dressed in jeans and a white linen shirt: a casual look that suited him, making a joke of the other men's contrived elegance. A gesture of defiance. A kind of I-don't-give-a-shit gesture to wealth and privilege, which made Daisy giggle.

The Italian frowned. "I am sorry? Did I make a joke?"

Daisy put her hand on his arm. "No, Antonio, it was me. Sorry. Something just popped into my mind that made me laugh."

Antonio smiled, looking even more handsome. "You're a funny girl, cara. A funny, beautiful girl." He put his arm around her and pulled her close. "Do you want to come with me to the Byblos? We could have dinner and then dance at the nightclub. What do you say? This party is getting a little boring, no?"

She glanced at Liam. He hadn't spotted her yet. "I'd love to," she said to Antonio. "Why don't we go right now? I'm sure nobody will mind."

"They will all be in Les Caves later," he said.

"Les Caves?"

He looked at her as if she was deranged. "Les Caves du Roy. You, know, the club."

Daisy forced a laugh. "Oh yes, Les Caves. I wasn't paying attention. Sorry."

"So, shall we go?"

Daisy shot a look across the terrace. Liam was talking to a man with white hair to whom she had been introduced earlier—a TV producer with the ABC network. Probably an important contact. He wouldn't notice her if she slipped away quietly. She smiled and nodded at Antonio.

"Yes, why not? I just want to…to powder my nose first. If I can find the ladies' room," she added with a laugh.

"Oh, but that's not necessary," he said and pulled her close again. "I have plenty of that," he muttered in her ear and patted the left side of his white linen jacket. "Got some earlier. The very best stuff."

Daisy blinked and stared at him. "What?" Then it dawned on her. "No, no," she hissed. "Not *that* kind of powder. I don't do that stuff. Or any stuff."

He took a step back. "You don't? How do you get high then?"

Daisy lifted her half-full champagne glass. "This is enough for me. Gee, I'm silly enough without dope. Can't imagine being *on* something as well. I find all that other stuff very scary. Not to mention what it does to your nose."

The light went out of his eyes and he looked suddenly a

lot less interested. "I understand. Okay. Nice to meet you, Daisy." He turned and disappeared into the laughing, chatting, drinking crowd.

Daisy shrugged and drained her glass. Not her type. She was beginning to feel a little disoriented and dizzy. Time to leave. Too much champagne and too many canapés. Lying down was suddenly the only thing she wanted to do. Wobbling slightly, she pushed through the crowd, smiling and nodding, until she was nearly at the door, where she found Marianne, saying goodbye to departing guests.

She turned to Daisy. "Are you leaving? But we're going onto supper at the Byblos later. Maybe you'd like to join us? We'll go on to Les Caves for dancing after that. Great fun."

"Ah no, thanks all the same. I'm a little tired," Daisy said, trying not to slur. How many glasses of champagne had she drunk? "Must go and lie down for a bit."

Marianne looked suddenly concerned. "Are you feeling all right? You look a little pale."

"Yeah, that's it. I'm feeling quite pale. I mean, I have a bit of a headache. Thanks for the drinks and the nosh. It was fab."

"Thanks for coming," Marianne said with a warm smile. "See you soon, I hope. You live at the Villa Alexandra, is that so?"

"I certainly do," Daisy said.

"I'll give you a call. Maybe we can have lunch?"

"That would be terr...turri...nice," Daisy said. She waggled her fingers in what she hoped was a cheery wave. "Must run. Byeee." And with that, she left Marianne and picked her way through the vast rooms, until she got to the hall, where she slipped on the marble. She would have crashed to the floor if a strong hand under her elbow hadn't pulled her up.

"Steady, princess" said a voice in her ear. "We wouldn't want to make a show of ourselves, would we?"

Daisy looked up at the man. "Nah, we wouldn't. Especially not you, Liam," she giggled. "Thanks for helping me. These floors sure are slippery."

"Very. Especially when one has drunk rather a lot of champagne," he drawled.

"Yes, I think I must have. It was an accident. They kept topping up my glass."

"Of course," he said sarcastically. "I hope you're not driving."

"Course not," she said and pushed at him. "That would be dangerous. I walked here. I live very close."

"I'll take you home." They had come to the bottom of the steps, Liam still holding onto Daisy's arm. "Where's your house?"

Daisy peered into the dark night. "That way," she said and pointed to the left. "Or maybe thataway," she slurred and pointed in the opposite direction. Where was the house again? "It's called…Villa Aly…uh…Aless…something."

"Villa Alexandra? I know where it is. The cube-like thing on top of the hill?"

"That's *it*! You're awfully clever."

"I know. But I think we'll take my car. I can't lug you around in the dark like this."

Daisy nodded several times. "Oh, yes. A car would be good here."

"I'm parked over there," Liam said and led Daisy out through the gates and down the narrow street until they came to a stop beside his Ferrari. He pushed her up against the car, holding her upright with one hand, while he took the car key out of his pocket and pressed the remote.

Daisy jumped as the car made a noise and a light flashed. "Oops, your car said something."

"It does that." Liam opened the passenger door and manoeuvred Daisy inside, lifting her legs and placing her feet on the floor once she was in the bucket seat. "There. Put on the seat belt while I get in, will ya."

"Suuuure," Daisy chanted, fumbling with the belt. "Anything for you, darling Liam." After a few tries, she managed to get the buckle in and click it in place. "This is a very gorgeous, fabulous car. Is it a Ferrari?"

"Yes," Liam grunted as he eased into the driver's seat.

"Ooooh," Daisy sighed, caressing the soft leather. "I've never been in a Ferrari before."

Liam stared at her. "Really? I would have thought a rich party princess like you, would have seen more Ferraris than I've had hot dinners."

Daisy shook her head from side to side. "No, no, no. I'm not a princess. Not of royal blood at all, at all, as you Irish people say."

"Just rich, then," Liam said.

Daisy nodded. "I must be. I mean, look at my dress. And—" She held up her evening bag. "This Prada thingy. Must mean I'm rich, mustn't it?"

"I suppose."

Daisy peered at Liam. "You think so?" She suddenly remembered her conversation with Molly. "What did she say? Molly, I mean. About me?"

"Nothing much."

"Oh, but…I told her some stuff about me."

"Molly's not the kind who'd blab about something a friend told her in confidence. So your secrets are safe, if that's what it was about."

"Phew. That's good to know."

"I see you're wearing the necklace you bought from Molly."

"Yes. It went like magic with the dress." She let out a little giggle. "Someone even asked which designer made it, so I said 'Molly of New York', he-he, and she believed me. Isn't that funny?"

"Hilarious." Liam rolled his eyes and then started to laugh. "Jesus, you're one mad woman. I'd better get you home, though." He hit the starter button on the dashboard, pressed the accelerator, and the car roared down the street and up the hill.

"Weeeeee!" Daisy shouted. "This is great!" Then she clapped her hand to her mouth. "Gee, not so fast. I feel a little…"

The car screeched to a halt. Liam turned to her with a worried look. "You're not going to—?"

Daisy shook her head and took a deep breath. "No. I feel better now. Just a little queasy. I won't throw up all over your nice car."

"I'm more worried about the dress."

"Me too. But 'sokay. I won't puke on it, promise."

"Good. In any case, we're here."

Daisy peered out. "Where?"

"Villa Alexandra. Where you live."

Daisy looked up at the house. "I live here? Gee whiz."

"You do."

"Oh. Okay." Daisy put her head on Liam's shoulder. "You're awfully good-looking, you know. You want to come in for a nightcap?"

"No, but I think I should help you inside all the same."

"That's what they all say." Daisy threw her arms drunkenly around Liam's neck. "You can carry me, if you like. That would be so romantic, dontcha think?"

Liam peeled her arms off. "It would if we were both sober."

"What? One of us is drunk? Who? Not me, I'm just a little tipsy."

"You're more than that."

"No I'm not," Daisy argued and tried to put her arms around him again. "Just a little tired. Need to go to bed. It's very big. Big enough for two. Wouldn't that be nice? You and me in bed? I'm very good in bed, you know. Or bad, I mean," she added with a cackle.

"I bet. Come on, let's get you inside. How do you open the gate? Is there a code?"

"No." After a little fumbling with the clasp, Daisy managed to open her bag. "There's a thing here to open it. A remote." She pulled out a key ring with a leather tag. "You press this and then, bingo, it opens."

Liam took the remote, pressed the tag and the gates slid open. He manoeuvred the car inside and turned off the engine. "The doors are massive. How do you open them? Another remote?"

"No, a code," Daisy mumbled. "She rummaged in her bag again, produced a card and handed it to Liam. "Here's the number. I can't even see it, so you'll have to do it."

"Great. I'll go open them and then I'll come back and help you up the steps."

"Fabulous," Daisy said and passed out.

Chapter 9

When Daisy woke up, she knew immediately she was in a strange bed. The room was vaguely familiar, but the sun streaming in through the large windows blinded her. Her head throbbed and her tongue felt like sandpaper. She shielded her eyes with her hand and looked around the room. *Why am I here? What happened last night?* She had a vague recollection of having drunk too much champagne and being driven home in a strange car. There was a man with her, who kept asking her questions. Then she blacked out, coming to briefly as she was lugged upstairs and then someone threw her on a bed—that bed. He must have put her into bed and pulled the covers over her.

But the dress? What happened to the dress? Daisy lifted the bedclothes and peered at herself. No dress, just her underwear. Where was that dress? Her hand still shielding her eyes, she looked around the room and saw the dress hanging on the back of the door. It looked okay. Someone must have taken it off her before she was put to bed. Someone? A man? Did he...had they? No, that would have been terrible. Having sex and then forgetting all about it. God, who was that man who brought her home last night? Was it that Italian with the long eyelashes? Or the bald guy who complained about not getting an acting job? Or...

Daisy closed her eyes and tried to remember. Opened them again and looked around once more. It slowly registered where she was. The master bedroom. She was in the master bedroom on the big bed, where *he*…who? Then suddenly, it all came back to her. Liam Creedon. He must have carted her upstairs when she passed out. Would he have—? She shook her head, wincing at the pain. No. Didn't look like the kind of man who would… Knowing she had probably been behaving like a drunken slut, Daisy blushed, thinking that he had taken her dress off and seen her like that, in underwear no bigger than a couple of postage stamps. And why had she worn the old bra with a safety pin holding up one of the straps? Not a prude by nature, Daisy still felt a stab of embarrassment. The thought of meeting him again made her cringe. She lay back and closed her eyes, but the pain in her head was worse than ever. *Better get out of here. Find painkillers and drink water. Lots of it.*

Her head throbbing, she crawled out of bed and managed to close the curtains. The light was now nearly bearable. But it was best to get out of there before Olivier found out. Daisy smoothed the bedclothes and managed to get the bed to look nearly as pristine as before. She inspected the dress. Just a little crease here and there but no major damage. She hung it back in the walk-in wardrobe, grabbed her handbag and was about to tiptoe out of the room when she spotted her phone on top of a scrap of paper with something scribbled on it on the bedside table. She picked up the note and read the short message.

Hope you feel okay when you find this. You were pretty drunk, so I pulled off the dress and just dumped you into bed. The hangover should be spectacular. See you around,

Liam

Daisy sighed and rolled her eyes, which hurt like hell. Typical. Such concern and sympathy. But at least he had helped her get home. Hopefully, he would forget about her drunken advances. She shuffled down the corridor to her own bedroom, where the shutters were closed and was blissfully cool and dark. She rummaged around in her drawers until she found two paracetamol tablets at the bottom of her bag of toiletries. She washed them down with a glass of water from the crystal jug on the bedside table and then glugged down two more glasses. Finally, she collapsed on top of the bed. Peace at last. She closed her burning eyes and fell asleep.

An hour later, something woke her up. She looked around and listened. What was that? A sound? No, more like a feeling, a scent in the air, something *different*, suddenly. There was someone else in the house. She lay there for a while, trying to gather enough strength to get up. She listened again. What was that sound? A snuffling and whining and then the soft murmur of a woman's voice. It was coming from the room opposite Daisy's. Come on, she said to herself, get up and find out.

She scrambled out of bed, threw on her bathrobe, grabbed her phone to be ready to call the police, marched across the corridor and threw open the door to the other guestroom.

"Who are you and—" She stopped and stared. A woman with black hair streaming down her back was sitting up in bed, cuddling Ivan and Bess.

Daisy didn't know what to do. She lifted her phone and punched in 112, the French emergency number. Ready to hit the call button, she shouted, "Don't move, or I'll call the police!"

"NO!" the woman shouted. "Don't call anyone. I can explain, I swear,"

"Yeah? Come on then, and make it snappy," Daisy ordered, glaring at the woman.

"I am Irina. The wife of the owner of the house. *This* house," she said in broken English.

"Yeah? Can you prove it?" Daisy said, feeling calmer. The woman looked exotic but not dangerous. In fact, she was beautiful in a theatrical way. Her hair was jet-black hair and her hooded green eyes were surrounded by long thick eyelashes. She was very pale and looked as if she had been through a huge ordeal. The dogs pressed up against her, licking her face, looking as if they had finally been reunited with the person they loved most in the world.

Then Daisy relaxed. The dogs not only knew this woman, they loved her.

"It's you," she said. "The owner of this house."

The woman nodded. "*Da*. That is what I said. It is me. Irina Kedrova." She made a gesture toward the bed. "Please. Sit. Close the door quietly. I do not want the butler to know I'm here."

"Olivier? He never comes up here," Daisy said and sank down on the bed. She patted Bess, who ignored her.

Irina nodded. "That is good. But you…you are Daisy, the house-sitter, yes? Belinda told me about you."

"Yes. I am. But…I mean…" Daisy put her hand to her head. "I'm sorry but I have a bit of a headache. And my brain doesn't seem to be working very well. Too much champagne last night."

Irina smiled and shook her head, making a 'tut tut' noise "Champagne is not a good way to get drunk. Vodka is much better. No hangover."

"I wasn't actually *trying* to—" Daisy stopped. "Never mind. Why are you here? I thought you weren't coming until the beginning of August."

Irina sat up and grabbed Daisy's arm. "Nobody must know I am here," she hissed. "*Nobody*. Is that clear?"

Daisy nodded and tried to pull away from the woman's iron grip. "Yes."

"Promise?" Irina's eyes bored into Daisy's.

"I swear."

Irina let go of Daisy and lay back against the pillows. "Good. But if you don't keep your promise, I will tell on *you*."

"Tell who what?"

Irina smiled sweetly. "I saw you come home last night, wearing my dress. You were at a party, no? A party I was invited to?"

Daisy squirmed. "Yes," she mumbled.

"And you pretended to live here and that you have a lot of money?"

"Kind of." Daisy dropped her gaze. "It was just for fun. I was bored. I didn't mean to deceive anyone."

"You did not mean it. But you did it anyway."

"I'm sorry," Daisy mumbled.

Irina pointed at Daisy. "That's very beautiful. Is it mine?"

Daisy touched her neck and realised she was still wearing Molly's necklace. "No. It's mine. A friend made it."

"A very clever friend. But we were talking about me. And you. I'm sure you don't want anyone to know the truth. Especially the handsome young man who brought you home."

"No," Daisy whispered, trying not to think of the charade she had played at the party the night before. "Please, I won't tell anyone about you. But why?"

Irina sat up again and smoothed the front of her black lace nightgown. Her slim arms and straight back hinted at a very fit body.

"It's like this," she said. "I am here in France without a visa. We went to London, just after buying this house and organising the furnishing and decor. Then we went to Russia to see family. But then, when Putin went all silly in the Ukraine, many of the European Union countries organised a blockade against Russians, refusing them residency or even a tourist visa. I didn't want to stay in Russia. My husband supports Putin and his regime, but I hate it. He has ruined my country. I have been talking about my hatred of all that man is doing. So this has been very embarrassing for my husband, and he told me I had better go to France and stay here. But then the blockade. Impossible to get back in. But I had to get back to my lovely new house and my babies." Irina hugged Bess, who licked her face. "And I finally succeeded."

"How did you manage it?" Daisy asked, trying to take it all in.

"Long story. I took a train from Moscow to Lithuania. Then I bought a car and drove all over Eastern Europe, into Hungary, then I had to hike across the mountains to Austria, from where I managed to get into Switzerland and then…" Irina sighed. "I hid on a tourist bus going into France. It was a big risk, but nobody noticed me. I arrived in Nice last night and took the train to Saint-Maxime, where I got on the very last boat across the bay to Saint-Tropez. It was dinner time, so the streets were quiet. I waited until you were gone and I could see the butler leaving."

"I guess he'd recognise you if he saw you."

"No, he wouldn't. He has never seen me. Belinda hired him after we left. Anyway, when I saw it would be safe, I went inside and got my darlings out." Irina shot an angry look at Daisy. "Why were they locked in?"

"Because I went out. I didn't want them roaming all over the house. But when I'm here, they're not locked in. And I do walk them three times a day. I had to be careful because Belinda told me to keep the dogs locked in all the time. It seemed a bit cruel, though."

Irina sighed. "Typical. That Belinda hates dogs. Just like my husband."

"Why did you sleep here and not in the master bedroom?"

Irina smirked. "Someone was already in there."

"Oh." Daisy blushed. "Sorry. It was an accident."

"Nice accident. Very handsome man. But he left very soon." Irina peered at Daisy. "Was it one of those, how do you say—quickies?"

"No," Daisy protested. "It wasn't like that at all. He was—"

"That's not important now," Irina interrupted. "I need to talk about me and my problem. You must understand that if the police find me here with no visa, I'll be arrested and deported."

"Yes of course. I'll make sure nobody knows about you. You need me to hide you here in the house?"

"In a way, yes," Irina agreed. "But I won't need to hide completely. I just have to be very careful."

Daisy nodded, still staring in disbelief at the exotic woman. She couldn't put a finger on it, but she had an odd feeling Irina wasn't telling the whole truth.

* * *

At breakfast later, still suffering from a pounding headache and slight nausea, Daisy managed to sip a cup of black coffee and nibble at a croissant. The umbrella and dark sunglasses helped to ease her sore eyes from the glare of the sun. She glanced up at the shuttered window, behind which Irina had gone to sleep again, the dogs at her feet. They needed their walk, but the thought of getting into a car and walk around in the woods in the heat seemed too much to endure. Maybe they could just have a short walk in the little field? And what about Irina? She had asked Daisy to smuggle up some food for her later.

Daisy was still trying to get her head around what had happened earlier, when Olivier appeared at her side.

"There is someone to see you," he murmured, and looked behind him. Daisy could see the figure of a man hovering under the awning at the French doors.

Daisy squinted at the figure. "Who is it?"

"A Mr Creedon, mademoiselle."

Liam. What was he doing here? "Oh, okay. Tell him to join me," Daisy said with a sinking feeling. Why did he have to appear, when she was pale and bleary-eyed wearing no make-up and still in her robe? Typical.

Olivier nodded at Liam, who strode across the sunlit terrace, looking annoyingly cheery. "Hi there, princess. How are we this lovely morning?" he said. He pulled out a chair and sat down opposite Daisy.

"Good morning," Daisy mumbled. "Please sit down."

"Thank you. Knew you'd invite me to join you." He scanned the table. "This looks delicious. Croissants and fruit and cheese and ham and—"

Daisy pushed her sunglasses up her nose. "Please. Stop. I'm not feeling very well."

"I can imagine." Liam nodded at Olivier, who had just arrived with another cup and plate. "Thanks, mate. Very considerate." But Olivier had glided away without replying.

"Quiet chap, isn't he?"

"He would be," Daisy drawled. "He's the butler."

"Of course. The butler. How posh." He looked around, at the house that towered above them and down the lawns where the sprinklers were making their usual noise. "So who owns this house? You?"

"Yes," Daisy said. "I do."

"How come you have so much money?"

"None of your business. But since you ask, my dad left it to me."

"Wow." Liam looked impressed. "How did he make all that money?"

"Oil," Daisy said without a moment's hesitation. Lying was suddenly so easy. Once she had started, it was difficult to stop. "Why are you asking all these questions?"

"Just curious." He peered at her. "You look a little pale around the gills. Not surprising considering you drank several litres of champagne last night."

"I don't want to talk about last night."

"I can imagine. But you probably don't remember much about it. Especially the last bit."

"That's the problem," Daisy said and picked up her cup.

"I do remember. Could we forget about it? Why are you here anyway?"

Liam poured himself some coffee from the silver coffee pot. "Not to remind you about last night. I have a proposition."

Daisy looked into her cup. "I didn't mean it," she mumbled.

"Mean what? Oh, about that charming invitation to take you to bed? Of course you didn't mean it. Not that it wasn't very tempting. You looked awfully cute all mussed up and amorous. Not to mention nearly naked."

"Shut up."

"Okay." Liam picked up a slice of ham and stuffed it into his mouth. "So," he said when he had swallowed his mouthful, "this is what I was going to suggest…"

"I don't want to hear your suggestions," Daisy snapped. "Whatever it is, I know I won't like it."

Liam sighed. "Will you at least listen?"

"Sure. How can I help it?"

"You can't, except if you stuff your fingers in your ears." Liam leaned his elbows on the table and looked at Daisy. "This isn't about me, it's about Molly. I've thought of a way you could help her sell her jewellery. Of course, she's selling it now in a small way, but I'd like her to make it big. I'm sick of seeing her trundling to the market every Sunday and working so hard for very little. I think her stuff is fantastic and deserves to be noticed and sold everywhere. Don't you?"

Daisy met his gaze, touched by the look she saw there. "Yes, of course. I told her so. And that necklace I wore yesterday got a lot of attention."

"'Molly of New York,'" Liam said.

Daisy felt her face flush. "That was just a lie I told for fun."

"Why not make it true?"

Daisy frowned, the remnants of her headache muddling her thoughts. "How do you mean?"

"Why not wear her pieces to all the parties you go to? I have a lot of them in the safe in my house. You could team them with the designer clothes you wear. Tell your rich friends they were made by Molly of New York." Liam drew breath and leaned back. "What do you think?"

Daisy stared at him as she considered his suggestion. It would have been a brilliant idea if she really had been the rich 'princess' he thought her to be. But more parties? She hadn't planned to go to any more of them. And the one the night before hadn't been as much fun as she imagined it would be. In any case, would Irina allow her to wear the clothes and go to more parties?

"I'll think about it," she said after a moment's reflection.

His face darkened. "I suppose you prefer to wear your own diamonds and pearls." He got up. "Forget it. It was just an idea."

"Don't stomp off in a huff," Daisy ordered. "Sit down. I haven't said I don't like it, have I?"

Liam sat down again. "You didn't exactly scream with excitement either."

"Oh please, I have a headache. I don't feel like screaming." Daisy pinched the bridge of her nose. Everything was getting very complicated all of a sudden. Irina upstairs in hiding. The dogs in urgent need of a walk. And now this idea Liam had just put before her. It required careful planning and maybe some major sucking-up to that strange woman upstairs.

"Come on. Spit it out," Liam ordered. "What do you think of my idea?"

Daisy sighed. "It's a good idea, and yes, why not give it a go? But you need to speak to Molly first."

"I already have."

"What did she say?"

"She wasn't too keen on it at first, but then when I explained what a great opportunity it would be, she agreed.

Actually, I think she's quite excited about it." He took a croissant from the plate and got up. "Have to go. I have a deadline and lots of painting to do too."

She looked up at him. "Painting?"

"Yes. I'm doing up the house little by little. It was a total wreck when I bought it, but I'm slowly getting it back to what it was. On the inside, anyway. It needs a new roof and the façade has to be redone. That involves builders and scaffolding, so I'm going to wait until autumn to do it. But the painting jobs and the new kitchen I'm doing myself. Now that Molly and Tommy and his dog are out of the way for a while, I can make a mess and not worry about them stepping into paint."

"Sounds like fun."

"Not to someone like you, of course. I bet you've had an army of decorators here. I walked through the living room. It's amazing."

"It's not finished yet," Daisy said, remembering with a dart of panic that the dining-room furniture was going to be delivered later that day. "Lots more to be done still."

"I bet." He moved away. "I have to go. Thanks for breakfast. Let me know when you want to come and get the stuff."

"Stuff? Oh, the jewellery you mean. Okay. I might swing by later today on my way home from the doggy walk."

"Great. I'll be there. See you later." He nodded at her, and still chewing on the croissant, strolled back across the terrace and into the house.

Daisy looked at his departing figure. A difficult man to figure out. He seemed hostile and contemptuous one minute, warm and caring about his family the next. And when he wasn't teasing her, he was quite nice to talk to. But there was something in his demeanour that hinted at a very private person. Someone who didn't like people to get too close. Maybe it was because of the loss of his wife? Daisy calculated it would have been four years since her death.

Probably a very short time for such a loss. It had taken her a long time to cope with the death of her dad, and she knew there would always be a sadness about it, a kind of longing and regret about what could have been. She wondered if she would have left New York if he hadn't died, if she would be drifting from one job to the next without any real ambition to do something better. Would her relationship with her mother have been different? There was no way of knowing and useless to dwell on what could have been.

Daisy finished her coffee and drank some orange juice but couldn't face anything else on the table in front of her. She got up and walked across the scorching terrace to get away from the heat and the relentless sun. Irina was waiting upstairs and was probably very hungry. Remembering her promise to take her some food, Daisy retraced her steps and loaded the tray Olivier had left with what remained of the breakfast. On her way upstairs, she collected the morning's post and took it upstairs for Irina. She glanced at the envelopes. More invitations. Would she be able to go to any of those parties? It all depended on that strange Russian woman upstairs. She seemed reasonably friendly, but there was an edge to her that made Daisy nervous. Best not to annoy her until they knew each other better. But as she entered the bedroom carrying the tray, she found Irina sitting up in bed with a laptop, tears streaming down her cheeks.

Chapter 10

Daisy put the tray on the little chest of drawers by the window and opened the shutters a crack.

"What's wrong?" she asked, as Irina kept sobbing.

"This," Irina said and turned the laptop around.

Daisy looked at the strange letters on the screen. "Sorry, but I don't read Russian."

Irina smacked her forehead. "Of course. I'm so stupid. This is an e-mail from Alexei, my husband. He is divorcing me."

Daisy sank down on the bed. "Oh no. That's awful. I'm so sorry."

"Yes, it—how do you say in your country—sacks?"

"Sucks. And it totally does," Daisy agreed. "Big time."

"He wants to get rid of me, I always knew that. But not that he'd want to marry that little bitch he has been sleeping with. I knew all about it, but I thought it was just a little affair that would end very soon. She is twenty-one and very cute. And very clever. She is from the Czech Republic and has a university degree in economics. I'm sure she knew all about his money before they even met. But once she got him into bed, he was in her power." Irina sighed and wiped her face with the sheet. "He got rid of me like an old shoe."

"So, what are you going to do?" Daisy asked. "Do you have to leave this house? And what about me?"

Irina sighed deeply. "Alexei is very generous. He is giving

me the house here and the apartment in London. Also a very big allowance or whatever you call divorce money."

"Alimony."

Irina nodded. "Yes, that's it. So I'm going to stay. I will still have to hide, as I have no visa, but this way, I can look around for a nice Frenchman to marry me, and then I'll be French and can stay here legally."

Daisy couldn't help laughing. "You make it sound like buying a pair of shoes. Where are you going to find a nice Frenchman?"

Irina stared at Daisy. "They're not nice?"

"Not usually. But maybe I've been unlucky."

Irina peered at her. "A Frenchman was not nice to you?"

Daisy shrugged and picked up the tray. "Not very, no. But never mind me." She put the tray on the bedside table. "Here, have some breakfast. It might make you feel better. You must be very upset about your divorce."

Irina nodded. She picked up a piece of bread and slathered it with apricot jam.

"I was. I cried and cried when I got the news. But then I realised this makes me free. Alexei and I were not that happy, really. I married him for the money, but then I discovered what kind of man he was. Selfish. Cruel. Vain. He didn't want children...that's why I had to have dogs." Irina flung back the bedclothes on top of the dogs, which made them jump up and bark. "Be quiet my darlings," she said and got out of bed, stretching her back and surveying the tray. "I must eat some more and have some coffee. And then we make plans, yes?"

"Why don't I take the dogs for a walk? You could get dressed, and then we'll see what we can come up with," Daisy suggested. "There's some mail there for you, too."

"Very well." Irina bit off a piece of bread. "We have to decide what to do about that butler," she said through her mouthful.

"Yes," Daisy agreed. "We'll have to tell him about you otherwise you're stuck up here. But I have no idea if he can be trusted."

"Oh, we'll just give him money," Irina said. "Or the other solution would be to fire him."

"Oh no," Daisy said, appalled. "We can't do that. He's been through so much. The war in Eritrea and seeing his whole family killed."

Irina looked thoughtfully at Daisy. "That's very bad. I will not fire him. We can tell him that I'm your friend and that I have problems with my husband. That's all he needs to know."

"Okay."

Bess suddenly jumped off the bed, followed by Ivan. They both ran to the door, whining. "They need to pee," Irina said. "You take them, yes?"

"Of course. I'll just take them down to the little field, and when I come back we'll make plans."

Irina nodded. "Yes. Plans. There is much to discuss." She picked up the pile of envelopes. "You go with my babies." She glanced out the window. "And on the way, you can deal with the butler. He's down there now. Whatever you tell him will decide my fate."

* * *

When Daisy was dressed, she made her way downstairs, the dogs at her heels. She spotted Olivier cleaning the pool and nodded at him.

"I need to talk to you," she said. "But the dogs need to be walked first."

"Yes, mademoiselle. I know," Olivier replied, not elaborating on what it was he knew. Daisy realised she had to tell him what Irina had suggested. There was no other way.

He was waiting on the terrace when she came back. He had tidied away the pool-cleaning equipment and stood there, his tall elegant figure outlined against the blue sky. Daisy suddenly felt a little awestruck. He was not someone one would lie to.

She stopped and let the dogs off the leads, watching as they scampered through the living-room door and raced upstairs to rejoin their mistress.

"They're allowed," she said.

Olivier nodded. "Yes. Maybe it's better for them."

Daisy cleared her throat. "I have to tell you," she said. "About—"

He nodded. "The woman upstairs?"

Her knees suddenly weak and her head still aching, Daisy sank down on one of the loungers beside the pool.

"Yes." She paused, and then found she couldn't tell him the truth. It was too risky. "A friend," she said instead. "She's just broke up with her husband and is terribly upset. She came last night and asked if she could stay here for a while."

Olivier opened the umbrella over Daisy's head. "The sun is hot." He stepped back. "A friend, you say?"

"Yes. She needed somewhere to stay. She doesn't want anyone to know where she is, so…"

Olivier nodded. "I understand. We have to keep her presence a secret. I will not tell."

"Yes. I didn't know if…" Daisy paused. "If I could trust you, to be honest."

"You can," Olivier said, looking slightly miffed. "Absolutely. I have had enough trouble of my own to know how it feels to be a fugitive. Rest assured, mademoiselle. I will never tell."

Daisy breathed a sigh of relief. "I believe you. And I trust you, Olivier."

He nodded. "Thank you, mademoiselle." He nodded, glided away and disappeared in his usual enigmatic way.

Daisy lay back on the lounger and closed her eyes. One problem solved. But what about the others? What would Irina think of lending out more of her designer wardrobe in order to help market Molly's jewellery? Would Olivier keep quiet? How long would Irina have to hide? The day had hardly started but it was already exhausting. Daisy closed her eyes and dropped off to sleep.

* * *

Despite Daisy's fears, Irina was intrigued by the idea of marketing Molly's work.

"Very good idea," she said, as she unpacked her bag and put her things away in the chest of drawers in the master bedroom. "If the jewellery is as nice as that necklace you wore last night, it should make people curious, I think."

"And you don't mind me going to the parties or wearing your clothes?" Daisy asked.

"Mind? No. I wouldn't have gone to the parties, anyway. I don't really know those people. We get invitations to everything because Alexei likes to invest in movies. Probably just so he can meet those beautiful women. And I hate the clothes. Not my style at all. But now he's not here and I can't go, it would be a pity to waste the opportunities, yes? And you can do something for me at the same time."

"What?"

"See if you can spot someone I can marry."

Daisy laughed. "You want me to find you a husband? How can I do that?"

Irina shrugged. "I don't know really. But just keep looking, all right?"

"Okay," Daisy promised, mentally rolling her eyes.

"What did you tell the butler?"

"Not much. Just that you're a friend who's broken up with

her husband. And that you wanted to hide for a while. So he said he wouldn't tell anyone you were here." Daisy laughed. "I was going to make up a story that you were from Lithuania or something, but I didn't have to in the end. I don't think Olivier wants to know."

Irina nodded. "The less he knows, the less he can tell. As long as we can trust him."

"I'm absolutely sure we can."

"Good." Irina opened the walk-in wardrobe and started to hang up the clothes that were in her bag. "I only brought a few things, but I don't need much if I'm not going anywhere." She turned and looked at Daisy. "You'll be wearing the party clothes. They will suit you much better than me. I never wanted them."

Daisy sat down on the bed. "You didn't? Why did you buy them?"

Irina shrugged. "I didn't. It was Alexei. He asked Belinda to buy clothes in my size to wear at parties during the summer. She didn't ask what I wanted. She just bought what was in fashion." Irina pulled a dark green silk kaftan with gold embroidery from her suitcase. "This is the way I like to dress. I bought it in Turkey. Very pretty, no?"

"It's beautiful and exotic," Daisy said and looked more closely at Irina, still dressed in the long, black, silk nightie. They were roughly the same height and weight, but the similarity ended there. The Russian woman's pale, nearly white skin and hooded green eyes were a sharp contrast to Daisy's golden complexion and brown eyes. "It will look very nice on you."

Irina looked pleased. She shook back her hair. "Yes, I think so. I like oriental clothes more than French designer outfits. So you're welcome to those things. And you can go to the parties and pretend you're me."

"I don't think that's a good idea," Daisy protested. "We couldn't be more different. Nobody would think I was you."

"No. We have to make up a new persona for you, then. Who did you say you were last night at that party?"

Daisy tried to remember. "I didn't really say anything. I just said my name was Daisy. Some of them seemed to think I was an actress, but even that was a bit sketchy. In fact, nobody really cared much what I did. Really weird."

"Those people are too preoccupied with themselves to be interested in other people. A beautiful woman in an haute-couture dress wouldn't be unusual. So you can just go on being Daisy, who lives in this villa. I don't mind you wearing the clothes. But there is one condition," Irina continued, looking at Daisy critically. "I want to pick the outfits."

"Of course."

"And I want to do the make-up too. You have to look dramatic and different." Irina studied Daisy. "You're pretty. But you look too ordinary."

"Well, today I must look like total crap." Daisy sighed and studied her tired face in the mirror.

"Yes, you do but still pretty." Irina grabbed Daisy by the shoulders and turned her to the light. "Much to do," she sighed after scrutinising Daisy's face. "But I can do it. I've had harder jobs than this." She extracted a pair of black cotton pants and a white silk tunic with gold embroidery from her bag. "I must get dressed." She quickly pulled off her nightie and put on a pair of silk knickers and a bra. "If you go and walk the dogs and then collect the jewellery, we can decide on an outfit for the party tomorrow night."

"Fine." Daisy glanced at Irina as she got dressed, trying to figure her out. Getting her consent to wear the clothes had been a breeze. But why did it seem a little too easy?

* * *

When Daisy arrived at Villa Mimosa later that day, she found Liam in the kitchen, his head in the oven, muttering to himself. She had meant to knock on the door, but finding it half open, she walked in, curious to see what this old house looked like inside and what Liam was doing to it. The entrance hall was small with creaking floorboards, peeling wallpaper, with a sagging chair leaning against the wall. A rickety staircase led to the upper floor.

Daisy stepped across the threshold into the next room, which must have been the living room. Here, the walls had been painted pale green. The newly sanded and polished floorboards shone in the light from the tall windows, and gossamer-fine curtains swayed in the gentle breeze. The view of the bay from there was lovely and somehow part of the room, as if someone had painted it and placed it just where it would fit. A sofa and two easy chairs covered in bright chintz stood against the far wall and there was a new rug, still rolled up and covered in plastic, beside them.

Daisy walked through another room which she guessed would eventually be the dining room, judging by the antique table and chairs piled up against the wall. The floorboards had been sanded and polished and the walls painted light cream, but there were no curtains, and the shutters were half closed.

She walked on along a short corridor and entered a large bright kitchen with oak cupboards and a big farmhouse-style kitchen table. She didn't see Liam at first and was startled by loud grunts. Then she spotted him, on his knees, in front of the stove, his head in the oven.

"Hello?" she said.

Liam swore loudly as he banged his head. "Shit!" He turned and glared at her. "What the—oh, it's you."

"Yes. I came to pick up Molly's collection."

He sat back on his heels. "Right. Sorry. I was changing the bulb in the oven and trying to fix a loose connection. But I think it's okay now." He was dressed in baggy shorts and a ripped T-shirt covered in paint stains. His hair stuck up at the back and there was a streak of soot across his cheek. He wiped his face with a rag. "I've been cleaning the oven on the back terrace. It's a kind of barbeque and pizza-oven affair. I cook my steaks there in the evening. Come and have a look. It's a nice place to sit at this time of day."

Daisy followed Liam out the back door and stepped onto a small paved patio. She looked around in surprise. It was an enchanting place, full of light and the sound of crickets and cooing of doves. It was surrounded by a hedge of flowering oleander bushes and shaded by a large umbrella pine, the scent of which mingled with wild thyme and lavender.

"What a gorgeous little space," Daisy exclaimed. "Like a magic outdoor dining room."

Liam pulled up a wicker chair with blue cushions from the seating arrangement beside the outdoor oven, where coals were smouldering under the grill.

"Take a seat, princess. I'll get you a cold beer."

"Perfect," Daisy sighed and relaxed in the chair. "If you had a cheeseburger too, then all my dreams would come true."

Liam stopped in his tracks. "A cheeseburger? I wouldn't have thought that would normally be on the menu for you."

"Ah, well, you have to slum it occasionally," Daisy drawled. "And right now, when I'm still a little hung-over, a cheeseburger would be the best cure."

"I see. Well, I have no cheeseburger. But I do have Irish pork sausages. I could grill a few. Would that do?"

Daisy sat up. "Oh my God, yes! I remember those sausages. Absolutely freaking delicious."

Liam laughed. "I didn't think an Irish pork sausage would meet with such delight. I think the charcoal is just about perfect, so shouldn't be long. Where are your dogs? You didn't leave them in the car on such a hot day?"

"No, I went back to the villa with them after the walk. Didn't want to have them here, annoying you."

"They wouldn't annoy me. I like dogs. I kind of miss Asta now that she's in Ireland with Tommy and Molly." Liam went into the kitchen to get the sausages and beer.

"It's a little early for dinner," he said, putting the sausages on the grill. "But I have a feeling you're hungry."

"Starving," Daisy said, as the smell of grilled sausage filled the air. "I didn't eat much for lunch." She drank from the bottle he had handed her and let out a discreet burp. "Oh, damn. Excuse me. Beer does that to me."

"Burp away, girl," Liam said and sipped from his bottle. "No need to stand on ceremony with me. I'm sure it's a break not to have to mind your Ps and Qs from time to time. Except, the higher you climb up the social ladder, the ruder people are. Especially the Brits. You'd think they'd be real gents, but they're quite the opposite."

"Really? I haven't come across that many Brits."

Liam looked startled. "That's strange, considering your, uh, station in life. I would have thought the daughter of an oil baron would have mixed only with the hoi polloi around here."

"Well, I've only just arrived," Daisy said airily, kicking herself. She had to remember to behave like a rich bitch around him. "I haven't really mixed with a lot of people here yet, apart from the party last night."

"When you staggered home drunk on the arm of a wild Irishman," Liam filled in. He looked at her, while the sausages sizzled on the grill. "Can't really figure you out. There's something that doesn't quite add up here."

"Don't try, then," Daisy retorted. "Are those sausages ready yet?"

Liam turned to check the grill. "Yes, they have that slightly blackened look." He lifted the sausages carefully onto a plate and put it on the table beside a basket of rolls. "Here. Put the sausages into the rolls. There's ketchup and HP sauce here, too. If you know what that is."

"Sure. It's that brown fruity sauce that's perfect with sausages and bacon." Daisy piled a bread roll full of sausage and added a large dollop of HP sauce. "Gorgeous," she said and crammed it into her mouth, dribbling sauce and fat from the sausage on her chin. "Abshlotley fantashtic," she mumbled through her mouthful. "Nuttin' like an Irish saushage."

Liam shook his head and laughed. "You sure are good at slumming it, babe."

"Thank you." Daisy swallowed, picked up her bottle and drained it.

"Another sausage?" Liam asked.

"Sure. Would love another one. They're so decadent somehow. You know that it'll make you fat and that it's crammed with chemicals and salt, but there's nothing like an Irish sausage, is there?"

"Nothing in the world," Liam agreed and wiped his greasy hand on his tee shirt. "How come you know so much about it?"

Daisy picked up another sausage. "I spent a few summers in Ireland when I was a child. My dad's family is from Dublin."

"Yes, so you said."

Daisy looked at him over her sausage.

"But what about you?" she enquired before he could ask any more questions. "What's your story?"

He shrugged and started to tidy away the food. "My story? Not much to tell. Farmer's son starts writing to relieve boredom in the winter months. It was a detective story set in Cork city. Then at the end of the winter, I found I had a story that wasn't half bad. So I sent it off to an agent, on the off chance he'd like it and maybe want to pitch it to a publisher. Didn't hear anything for over a month, so I guessed he didn't like it and shoved it in a drawer. Things got busy at the farm too, with lambing and calving, so it all slipped my mind until this agent phoned me out of the blue and said he wanted to represent me. I didn't really know what it all meant, but I signed the agreement with him. Not long after that, he pitched it to several of the bigger publishers and then there was an auction. It was sold to Random House for a six-figure sum. They also offered me a three-book deal. They wanted me to develop it into a series. So that's when the Seamus O'Shea series was born. Nearly fifteen years ago. The rest, as they say, is history."

"Some history," Daisy remarked. "And one of your books was made into a movie too."

Liam took Daisy's plate and stacked it under his. "Yes. And my agent's negotiating with the producers for another movie deal or a TV series, which I'd prefer. I'm writing the screenplay myself."

"Exciting," Daisy said wanting to find out more. She suddenly felt a need to know the man behind the success. "But you didn't say why you're here. Why you bought this house. Are you going to move to France?"

Liam stopped at the door on his way to the kitchen with the plates. "Yes. For no reason other than I love France. I've always wanted to live here but never did anything about it. Then, when we were here on holiday at Easter time last year, Molly found this house. I had a look, and although it was pretty wrecked, I saw the potential and how it could make a good home for the three of us. Well, two of us," he corrected himself. "Molly will want a place of her own one day. But right now, she's happy to live here and help me with Tommy. I…" He hesitated. "I find it hard to be alone." He looked down at the plates in his hands as if he didn't want to meet Daisy's eyes. Then he went into the kitchen, leaving Daisy sitting in the quiet space, listening to the doves, suddenly feeling an enormous sympathy for him.

She got up and followed him into the kitchen. "Maybe I should collect the stuff and get going? I'm sure you have work to do or something."

"You probably have to go to a party," he replied.

"Not tonight. But I think I'll have an early night all the same."

"Now that you've had dinner," he added and winked at her. "Bet you never expected it to be Irish sausages and beer."

She laughed. "Not exactly. But it was really good. Just what I needed." Daisy walked around the table to get to the door. "But if you could give me Molly's stuff, I'll—" she stopped as Liam put his hand on her arm.

"Don't go," he said. "It's not that late."

His touch made her shiver. That warm hand on her bare skin was more seductive than a thousand kisses. The look in his eyes was hotter than the fire in the grill outside. She was sure her eyes betrayed her attraction to him—and her fear. *Here we go again,* she thought. *The same old story. Attracted to hot man with a fierce temper and a mean streak.* She backed away. "I have to go. I can't—"

His hand fell and his eyes hardened. "I see. Not quite the gentleman, am I?"

"It's not that," Daisy protested. "It's just that I'm…I've just come out of a relationship and it was very painful. I'm not ready to jump into something else. Not ready to be hurt again," she ended lamely.

His eyes softened. "Who said anything about a relationship? I think you're galloping ahead here. We've only just met. Okay, I've seen your hot body in skimpy underwear, and I don't mind telling you I was pretty tempted. Who wouldn't be? But you were out for the count and I have my own rules about that. I also like the woman to be conscious," he added with a wink.

Daisy couldn't help laughing. "Yeah, that makes it a lot more enjoyable."

He winked. "Sure does. Good that you laid the cards on the table. And believe me, a relationship isn't something I'd want either. Ever." He picked up the plates, opened the dishwasher and put them in. "Let's go and find Molly's stuff."

"Great." Daisy felt herself relax. The spell was broken, the tension in the air drifting away like a small cloud. "Let's go and have a look."

"It's in the safe."

Daisy followed Liam to a small room beside the kitchen, where he opened the door of a cupboard, behind which she saw a safe built into the wall.

"I had this put in when we came here. "Much better than having all your stuff lying around. There's a lot of petty crime around here. Big crime too, I'm sure. Houses get broken into all the time. Not that this house looks like someone rich lives here, of course."

"But you must have made a lot of money from your books. And the movie deal."

He shrugged. "I do okay. I bought the Ferrari with the advance from my last book deal. Stupid thing to do, but I always wanted one, so why not?" He extracted a box from the safe and handed it to Daisy. "Here, have a look. Pick a few pieces for now. No need to take the whole lot at once."

Daisy put the box on top of the cupboard and opened it. There were piles of little velvet pouches inside. "I'll look through them and see which ones I can use. I think there's a party tomorrow somewhere."

"The pool party at that Italian guy's house?"

"I think that's it."

"It would be casual, so bear that in mind. Well, casual to them, of course. Which means laid-back but expensive." He laughed and shook his head. "Who am I telling? You know all that stuff, don't you?"

"Sure," Daisy said and opened one of the velvet pouches and took out a pair of pendant earrings with aquamarines set in silver. "These are gorgeous. I can wear them on their own with a black top and white pants." She opened another pouch and pulled out a necklace with large jade stones set in gold, then another containing a pendant with a huge drop-shaped amethyst. "Beautiful," she said, stroking the stones. "I think these three will do for now. I'll take them with me."

Liam nodded. "Great choices." He paused for a moment. "I'm supposed to go the pool party too. I wasn't going to accept, but maybe you'll need an escort?"

Daisy glared at him. "Escort? I think I can manage to go to a party on my own, thank you."

"I know you can. But that party is hosted by Antonio Lorenzo. You met him last night, I'm sure. Tall smoothie with a girly face."

"I think I know who you mean," Daisy said, remembering the man who had offered her coke. "A bit of a sleaze."

"And the son of one of the wealthiest men in Italy. Not someone you should get close to."

"I know that too." Daisy sighed, tired of arguing. "But thanks for the offer. I wouldn't mind an escort, as you call it. You'd make a great fashion accessory if you clean yourself up."

"Gee, thanks." Liam grinned. "In any case, that would work two ways. If we pretend we're an item, it could help me fend off the attentions of the, uh, starlets who keep telling me they want to play the heroine in the next movie."

Daisy pouted. "Poor thing. Chased by gorgeous girls who'd do anything for an itsy-bitsy little walk-on part in a movie. Don't know how you stand it."

Liam laughed "It's tough. And many times they don't take no for an answer. That's why I need a prop, someone they'll believe I'd find attractive. You fit the bill perfectly."

"Gee, I'm flattered. But okay, why not? So we have to pretend to fancy each other, is that it?"

"If you can manage it, yes."

"It'll be tough, but I think I can pull it off without vomiting."

"I'll do my best to look amorous around you." He closed the safe. "All for Molly, right?"

Daisy nodded. "Anything for her."

"We'll pretend to be the hottest couple on the Riviera," Liam joked. But the look in his eyes told her he wouldn't have to pretend.

Chapter 11

"Smoky eyes," Irina said as Daisy sat in front of the dressing table mirror in the master suite. But we do the hair first, yes?"

Daisy nodded, looking back at Irina who, with a determined expression, took a handful of Daisy's hair and pulled it back. "I'm in your hands. Do what you like."

"I will," Irina said while she worked, pinning Daisy's hair into a simple knot at the nape of her neck. "You have a long neck. You shouldn't hide it. Look, it's nice like this, no?"

Daisy studied herself in the mirror and found she liked the severe hairdo. It made her eyes even bigger and revealed her cheekbones and her rather nice neck. "It's lovely. I've never worn my hair like this before."

"You should. It suits you. Now, close your eyes and don't look until I tell you."

Daisy obeyed and gave herself up to Irina's skilled hands. "How come you know so much about hair and make-up?"

"Before I married Alexei, I worked at the Bolshoi."

"As a ballerina?"

"No, as make-up artist. The Bolshoi is not just ballet, you know. It's also an opera house. I used to do the singers' make-up and the dancers also. My mother was the dresser of the famous Maya Plisetskaya. You have heard of her?"

"I think I've heard the name. Was she a singer?"

Irina smoothed foundation on Daisy's face. "No, she was

a famous ballerina. One of the greatest. Now, for the eyes. Keep them closed."

"Okay." Daisy could feel Irina applying liner and shadow on her eyelids, then mascara.

"Open them and look."

Daisy opened her eyes and gasped as she saw her face. She hardly recognised herself. Who was this glamourous woman with the dark, smoky eyes?

"Wow," she whispered. "I look—"

"Wonderful," Irina chortled. "Now, all we need are the clothes and earrings. The black silk top from Versace, I think. And the white palazzo pants from Armani."

"Yes," Daisy said, mesmerised by her image in the mirror. Irina hadn't applied lipstick, only touched her lips with nude lip gloss, which made her eyes all the more dramatic. She got up from the stool and went to put on the clothes Irina had laid out on the bed. First the black silk top that shimmered as she moved, followed by the wide-legged palazzo pants and then the strappy stiletto sandals. The finishing touch was the earrings, which Daisy put on carefully, leaning forward to see in the mirror properly. She stepped back for the full effect.

"Awesome," she murmured.

"Yes," Irina agreed with satisfaction. "Very good. The earrings are perfect. I have never seen jewellery like this before. It's unique." She smoothed the neck of the top and did up the tiny buttons at the back. "Oh," she said as she stepped back. "Forgot to ask. Do you know the code to the safe?"

Daisy stared at her. "You don't have it?"

"No, Belinda must have changed it before she left. And now she isn't replying to my messages or texts. I thought she might have given it to you."

"I have the code book in my room. In the safe. I'm sure it's there somewhere."

Irina brightened. "Yes! Of course. It must be there. Could you get it for me?"

"Sure," Daisy said and went to her room to open the safe. She quickly punched in the code and jumped as Irina looked over her shoulder. "You gave me a fright."

"Sorry." Irina scanned the contents of the safe. "What else is in there?"

"Just some of my stuff like my passport. Then the code book, a spare remote, a list of the artefacts in the living room, some instructions on how to open the garage door and—" Daisy paused as Irina grabbed both the code book and the folder with the instructions.

"I'll have a look at it all," she said.

"Great. I don't need it anyway, now that you're here."

"Of course not." Irina grinned. "I'm the boss now."

There was something in her eyes that made Daisy stiffen. A feeling of doubt flitted through her mind. What was Irina's real agenda?

* * *

Daisy forgot her doubts about Irina when she stepped outside the gates and saw Liam leaning against the newly washed Ferrari. In his blue linen shirt and beige chinos, his dark hair flopping into his bright-blue eyes, he looked like something out of an ad for Dolce and Gabbana male cologne: all tanned, designer stubble and brilliant white teeth in a cheeky grin. She stopped for an instant just to take him in and saw he was doing the same. Neither of them spoke.

Liam let out a long, slow whistle. "Holy mother."

"What's wrong?" Daisy enquired, adopting a model pose with her hand on her hip.

"Nothing at all, princess." Liam opened the passenger door. "Please step inside and I'll take you to the ball."

"Well, thankee very much," Daisy simpered and eased

herself into the bucket seat. Liam got in beside her and started the engine.

"Let's hit the road," he said, and they took off in a shower of gravel up the hill and along the winding back road to Ramatuelle village, which would take them to Antonio Lorenzo's home and the pool party.

The villa, an old vineyard château, stood on a hill above the vine groves just outside Ramatuelle. The setting sun bathed the pink stucco façade in a golden glow, and all the windows reflected the sunset, making it look as if the inside of the house was on fire.

"What a beautiful house," Daisy breathed. "It looks as if it's been standing here since time began."

Liam pulled up in front of the steps "I think it has. Or since the eighteenth century, anyway."

A man in a white jacket ran down the steps. "I'll park the car for you, monsieur," he said.

Liam opened the door for Daisy and helped her out. "Here," he said to the man, and handed him the keys. "Be gentle with her, will you?"

"Her?" Daisy asked. "Your car's a woman?"

"All cars are. This one is sleek and beautiful and quite temperamental. Reacts quickly and runs smoothly if handled with care. Not unlike you."

Daisy rolled her eyes. "Oh shit, that's so corny."

Liam took Daisy's elbow. "I'm a writer, remember. We're masters at the old cliché. Let's go and show off Molly's work and pretend we're hot for each other."

"I can tell it's going to be a fun evening."

"Shut up and smile—we seem to be on candid camera," Liam muttered in Daisy's ear as a man pointing a video camera at them came around the corner of the house.

"Hey, Liam," the man said. "This is for E News. Who's the hot woman?"

"It's a secret," Liam said. "All will be revealed soon. But

zoom in on her fantastic earrings. They're by Molly of New York," Daisy said, feeling that "New York" sounded a lot more glamorous that Ireland. "New, exciting designer."

The man pointed his camera at Daisy. "Gee, yes, they're really awesome."

"You'll see her new collection on the catwalks in August," Daisy said on a whim.

"What?" Liam muttered when the arrival of a Rolls Royce had pulled the photographer's attention away from them. "Was that a good idea?"

Daisy shrugged. "Why not? Might as well get the ball rolling."

"That should do it. But it's her jewellery that has to be the focus of attention tonight."

"I'll do my best."

Liam pulled her close. "Our love story should do it, don't you think?" he whispered in her ear before she could break loose.

It did. As Liam and Daisy walked around the house to the back terrace with the huge pool around which a large number of guests were drinking champagne and nibbling on tiny pieces of toast covered in caviar, all eyes were suddenly on them. Whether it was Liam's rugged handsomeness, her own striking appearance or the earrings, she couldn't tell. But as they approached, there was a communal murmur until everyone resumed their conversations.

Their host, Antonio Lorenzo, detached himself from a group of giggling bikini-clad starlets and walked toward them, his arms out, as if he was about to envelop them both in a group hug.

"My friends," he gushed. "Welcome."

"He's all yours," Liam said and disappeared into the throng.

"Gee, thanks," Daisy muttered, taking a step back

"Cara mia," Antonio said and swept Daisy into his arms. "How wonderful that you could come."

125

"Yeah, lovely," Daisy replied, her cheek pressed against his black silk shirt. Not that it was unpleasant to be hugged by this hunk. He had a fabulous body and smelled divinely of spicy men's cologne. But he was too much on the prowl, making it obvious he would have done anything to get her between his, no doubt silk, sheets. The thought that the sex would probably be spectacular flitted through her mind for a second before she pushed the thought away. *Don't go there, Daisy*, she chided herself. He had offered a little more than sex the last time.

He let her go and took a step back. "You look even more beautiful than the last time I saw you."

"Thank you. It's probably the earrings, don't you think?" she said and turned her head to show them off.

"Oh, yes," he said, but he wasn't looking at the earrings. "Is that man your…amore?"

"Uh, well…it's complicated."

He nodded. "I understand. It's an affair with much fighting, no?"

"Something like that." Daisy shrugged and smiled. "Irish men, you know?"

"Very much like the Italians," Antonio agreed. He pulled her close again. "If you get tired of fighting, let me know, eh?"

"I will," Daisy promised. "But now I need champagne. And I see some people I should say hello to," she added, having spotted Marianne, the hostess of the previous party waving at her. "If you'll excuse me, Antonio…"

He kissed her hand. "Only for now, bella. I will catch up with you later, no?"

"I have no doubt you will," Daisy said and winked at him as she moved off.

"Hi," Marianne said. "Lovely to see you again, er—"

"Daisy."

"Oh, yes, Daisy. You're a singer, right? Or was it actress?"

Marianne looked at her vaguely, playing with her platinum-blonde hair. "Love the earrings." She leaned forward to have a closer look. "Amazing work. Handmade?"

Daisy touched the earrings. "Yes. They're by Molly of New York. A new jewellery designer. Each piece is handmade and unique. There's only one pair of these in the whole world."

"Wow. Would this Molly make a pair for me?"

"I'm sure she would."

"You a friend of hers?"

"Associate," Daisy said. "I handle the marketing. And I model the prototypes. I wanted to invest in a new business, and this time I thought it would be nice to have a hands-on approach."

Marianne shot her an envious look. "Sounds like fun. And you're not married, are you?"

"Uh, no. Not at the moment," Daisy replied, whishing she had a script. It was hard to keep track of all the fibs she had told.

"You're dating that hot Irish guy, though? Liam Creedon?"

"Sort of. On and off, kind of," Daisy said vaguely. "We only just met, actually. But we hit it off straight away. Hate at first sight, really."

Marianne laughed. "I feel you're a very free spirit. You have your own money, of course. You don't have to suck up to rich men or have to worry your husband will leave you for someone younger."

"But you don't have to worry about that, surely?" Daisy asked, mystified. "I mean you're young and gorgeous and very nice."

Marianne sighed. "Young?" She leaned closer to Daisy. "Don't tell anyone," she whispered, "but I'll be forty-two next week."

Daisy blinked. Marianne didn't look a day over twenty-eight. "Wow. I would never have believed it. What's your secret?"

Marianne shrugged. "Secret? Facials, Botox and some nip and tuck here and there. Laser sometimes and IPL. All of that shit. I'm sick of it." She shot a glance at her husband, who was deep in conversation with another man at the far side of the pool. "Klaus doesn't know how much I've had done. He thinks it's all natural. Says I look amazing for my age. But I've seen him ogling other women lately. I'm his third wife. I'm sure he'll want a fourth one day. They all do." She sighed, suddenly looking sad. "If I was just after him for the money, I'd just take the alimony and run. But…I just can't. I'd rather die."

"Why?" Daisy asked, shocked by the pain in Marianne's eyes.

"Because I love him. Isn't that a hoot?" She let out a hollow laugh. "I'm in love with my husband. Pathetic, don't you think?"

Daisy didn't know what to say. A waiter interrupted them with a tray of brimming champagne glasses, and she grabbed one and emptied it in one go.

"What about him?" she asked. "Doesn't he say he loves you, too?"

Marianne sighed. "Not that often. Occasionally, when we're in bed. Other than that, no. But he's German and quite unemotional. Doesn't show his feelings much." Marianne sipped her champagne and looked out over the vine-covered hills. "I wish we could get away from here," she said wistfully. "I wish he'd come to Sweden with me and spend a little time alone with me. There is this little island in the Baltic, where my family has a summer house…"

"Have you asked him?"

"Yes, but he says he needs to be here to network and keep track of his business interests. He's a real workaholic." Marianne sighed. "I don't know why I'm telling you all this. But there's something about you that makes me think we could be friends."

Daisy put her hand on Marianne's arm. "Oh yes, me too."

Marianne's eyes took on new warmth. "Everyone needs a friend. Someone you know you can trust. Someone to have a good laugh with and tell secrets to without being afraid it would go any further. Difficult to find in this place, you know."

"I can imagine." Daisy reached out for another glass of champagne, but a hand on her wrist stopped her.

"Go easy on the booze, princess," Liam said in her ear. "We don't want to repeat what happened the other night, do we?"

Marianne looked intrigued. "What happened?"

"Oh, nothing," Daisy said with a shrug. "Liam got drunk and then he wasn't able to, you know, perform. Very sad, really. Happens to him quite often these days."

Marianne nodded. "Alcohol can do that to some men. But if you'll excuse me, I have to go and see if Klaus needs me." Marianne took a smartphone out of her evening bag. "Daisy, give me your mobile number. We must get together for a coffee soon."

Daisy rattled off her number and Marianne punched it into her contact list. "Thank you. I'll be in touch. Bye for now."

"Bye, Marianne," Daisy chortled. "I have to keep an eye on Liam and make sure he doesn't drink too much."

"Very funny," Liam muttered.

Daisy giggled. "I enjoyed it. Especially your face."

"Yeah, right. Have you been able to show off the earrings?"

"Yes. Quite a few women have said they'd love to see more of Molly's stuff. So I had this idea…"

"What?"

"First, why not have business cards printed with the link to Molly's website, where she'd have photos of her best pieces? It's already up but needs to be improved, which

shouldn't take long. I could do it if you like. I used to—"
Daisy stopped herself before she revealed that she had been
working in an estate agency and ran their website.

Liam made an impatient gesture. "Used to what?"

"Oh nothing. Just that I used to play around with graphics and stuff as a hobby. Web design and that kind of thing."

"You did? Could come in useful all right. Then what?"

"And then there could be a launch party and we'd invite
everyone around here we think would be interested. I've had
enough enquiries to make me think it would work."

"Launch party?" Liam said. "Where?"

"Oh, I don't know. Maybe your house?"

Liam stared at her. "My house? But it isn't finished, and
Molly and Tommy will be back tomorrow. That's a terrible
idea. How about your house? It's certainly big enough. You
could get a few of those wannabe actresses to model the
stuff around the pool. Get all your rich friends to come, and
throw a jewellery party. Must beat the spa-with-Botox gigs
the women do around here."

"What?" Daisy stammered. "My house? But..."

"But what?"

"Er, well, it's just that..." She tried to think of an excuse.
*But it's not my house and the wife of the Russian owner is
hiding upstairs*, she wanted to say. She suddenly felt tired of
the whole charade. What would he say if she told him the
truth? He would have spat in her face, probably and then
hate her forever and she would never see Molly or Tommy
again. "I'm having some work done at the house," she said
finally. "But you know what? I think Marianne would love
to host it."

"Not a bad idea," he said begrudgingly. "We'll float it all
to Molly when she comes back tomorrow. In the meantime,
go out there and do what you do best."

"And what would that be?"

"Flaunting your assets."

"I'm not going to dignify that with a response," Daisy said between gritted teeth.

"Thank God for that."

"Oh, shut up," Daisy said and broke away from Liam and his mocking eyes. Why did he get under her skin like this? Why was he so charming to everyone else? Why was it so hard to breathe when he touched her? She knew the answer but didn't want to delve into her heart any deeper. Better to lock up her feelings and stay cool. She looked ahead and smiled at a woman she vaguely recognised from the previous party. She joined the group and soon found herself chatting about fun trivial things like fashion and beauty and who had had what kind of plastic surgery, the latest marital break-ups and someone's interior-design disaster. Being an avid reader of gossip and fashion magazines helped Daisy fall into the conversations as if she was born to the world of glamour. It was fun to hear the backbiting and bitchy comments from these insiders. They revealed the ugly reverse side of the rich and famous. They also made her realise that in their world, you had to look out constantly for a knife in your back and there was no such thing as real friendship. Was that why Marianne was so miserable and lonely?

The sun disappeared and the sky darkened to a deep blue with pinpricks of stars. The sound of the crickets receded to a soft, distant chirping, and the warm breeze cooled hot bare skins and ruffled perfect hairdos.

"Have you had enough?" Liam sidled up beside Daisy as she was nibbling on barbequed chicken and salad. "I know I have. In fact if I have to stay much longer, I'll scream my head off or get horribly sloshed and start singing rude songs."

"I think I *have* had enough, actually. Anyway, it's always good to leave a party when it's in full swing."

Liam surveyed the scene around the pool and the chatting, drinking, eating crowd. "Seems to be the perfect moment, then. Everyone's happy. They'll no doubt decamp to the hot spots of Saint-Tropez later and dance the night away. Then they'll sleep with someone unsuitable, wake up in the wrong bed, nurse their hangovers and arrive at any of the swish beach clubs around noon, where they'll spend the day doing nothing until the next party. Rinse, repeat, ad nauseam, for the rest of the summer season."

"Gee, you make it sound such *fun*," Daisy squealed. "Why are you here then, if you hate it so much?"

"Because I have to be." He peered at her. "How much have you had to drink?"

She put her plate on a table. "Enough to punch you in the face if you get obnoxious."

He took her arm. "Let's get going, then. I'm sure Antonio will be disappointed when you leave. He looks at you as if he's you earmarked for his bed later on."

Daisy glanced across the patio and caught Antonio's eye. He winked at her.

"Yeah, and he also has the *best* coke on the Riviera, he told me. It enhances the whole sexperience, he said."

"Sexperience?" Liam laughed. "Did you invent that or did it just come out by accident?"

"You'll never know."

"May I use it?"

"Be my guest. And yes, let's go. I'm quite tired."

"Let's leave this sleaze-pit, then." He took her hand. "We'd better look as if we actually like each other or our cover will be shot. In any case, it's dark and you'll break your neck in those heels. Come on, let's get outta here."

"Sounds good to me," Daisy agreed, finding herself liking the feel of her hand in his. It was reassuring, sweet and very comforting.

Hand in hand, they made their way across the dark lawn and around the house to the front entrance, where, as if by magic, Liam's car was waiting.

"How did you do that?" Daisy asked.

"I told one of the waiters we were leaving, so he must have told the valet-parking guys. Antonio offers great service to his guests, I have to say."

Daisy sank into the bucket seat and yawned. "God, I'm tired. Take me home, James, and don't spare the horses."

"Yes, ma'am," Liam said and started the engine. He revved it up and took off down the hill at breakneck speed.

"I hope you didn't drink too much," Daisy shouted. "The cops around here are very strict."

"One glass of champagne, that's all. I don't even like the stuff but you have to be polite."

Daisy turned to him. "Polite? You? I didn't even know you could spell it."

"I'm very polite deep down." Liam pushed the foot on the pedal and the Ferrari roared around the bends.

"Is it wise to go so fast?" Daisy enquired, her stomach churning as she looked down at the sheer drop at the edge of the road. "I mean it's quite steep on this side."

"The roads are empty. Great time to do some serious driving. Don't worry, princess. I'm a good driver."

Daisy chewed on her lip. "Yeah, but…"

Liam wasn't listening. His eyes glittered and his hands tightened on the wheel as he took the sharp bends with great expertise. Daisy soon found she was enjoying the drive once she had put her fears to the back of her mind. She liked sitting in this beautiful car, watching Liam drive. He turned on the radio, and French hard rock thumped through the loudspeakers, adding to the buzz of the drive.

It was over all too soon. Liam slowed down once they reached the outskirt of Saint-Tropez, and he drove sedately through the quiet streets until he came to a stop in front of the gates of Villa Alexandra.

Catching her breath, her heart still thumping, Daisy looked at Liam. "That was fun, once I managed to swallow my heart."

Liam patted the dashboard. "Yes, this old girl goes like a rocket. Never disappoints."

"Thanks for tonight."

"No reason to thank me. You were the one who did all the work. More to come."

"I know. I'm going to look up Molly's website and see how we can improve it. I'll also see if I can get some samples of those business cards. I'll get started tonight."

"Why the rush? You can wait until tomorrow."

Daisy checked her watch. "But it's only eleven o'clock. I can put in an hour or two, no problem."

"You're very hard-working for a lady of leisure."

"I like having things to do."

"Admirable." Liam got out and opened the passenger door. "Get to work, then, Your Ladyship."

Daisy scrambled to get out of the low bucket seat and finally held out her hand. "Pull me out of this thing, will you? It wasn't made for tall people."

He took her hand and pulled her out. "Those long legs could be a problem in some situations." He didn't let go of her hand as she got out and pulled her close, so close she could feel his hot breath on her face. Their eyes locked. He touched the earrings. "Goodnight, a chuisle mo croi."

"What does that mean?" Daisy whispered.

"Look it up." Liam let her go and got into his car.

"See ya," he shouted above the roar of the engine and drove off.

Chapter 12

Daisy let herself into the quiet house and took off her shoes. She could see a strip of light under the door of the office and hear Irina talking to someone on her phone. She was probably organising her affairs after the divorce.

As Daisy padded across the hall, she heard Irina suddenly raise her voice. "Dimitri, I'm in charge here. Don't try to order me around. I know I can get all the information we need for the next job." Then she lowered her voice and Daisy couldn't hear the rest.

Mystified, Daisy made her way up the stairs. Who was Dimitri? And what was 'the next job'? Irina's English had also been a lot more fluent and precise than normal. Was she here for a different reason than she pretended? She could even be dangerous. Daisy felt tiny spiders of fear creep up her spine as the thought of Russians spies and KGB agents flitted through her mind. Then she shook herself mentally. That was silly. It wasn't some kind of spy movie. Irina probably had a lover and had to think of a way to get to him without being seen. Poor woman, she must have been going through hell. Daisy giggled. Irina was obviously the boss in that relationship. She did seem to be the dominatrix type too. Dimitri…wasn't that a Greek name? Probably a real hunk. Maybe some kind of toy boy?

A text message on her phone took Daisy's mind off Irina for a moment. It was from Flora. *Daniel, our second son, born early this morning. Big baby. Birth hell. Will be busy for a while. Flora xxx*

Daisy replied with a congratulatory note, telling Flora to get in touch when she wanted company. Smiling, Daisy went into her room and still wide awake, took out her laptop and put it on the antique desk by the window, sat down and switched it on. Molly's website soon came up and she studied it for a while. Yes, it was a little clunky and amateurish. Just a cheap WordPress thing anyone could put up. It had to be changed to look exclusive and special. She switched to stock-photo websites and other places on the Internet where she could find suitable designs for a new look. Molly's site had to show off her beautiful work and reflect the ancient Celtic art from which she took her inspiration: mystical, unique and romantic with a modern twist. Something the wealthy women she met would go wild about.

Daisy sat there into the early hours of the next morning, looking at thousands of images and designs, until she had put together a template of something she was happy with. It was a huge challenge: something all-absorbing and truly creative. Setting up the website for the agency had been fun, but this was a lot more than that. Sitting back, looking at what she had put together, Daisy felt a sense of pride. She suddenly realised she might finally have found the beginning of a career path.

* * *

Two days later, in the late afternoon at the old house, Molly looked at the page on the screen of Daisy's laptop.

"This is wonderful. I could never have done this myself."

Daisy nodded. "Well, you do need certain skills. I've done a few things like this before. Not professionally. Just for fun. But I'm thinking of setting up a business and doing this full-time."

Molly stared at her. "Business? But you don't have to work, do you? You're already wealthy."

"Yes, but doing something you love isn't work. And setting up a business is a huge challenge. Beats sitting on my ass on the beach all day. And I want to do this for you. I love your work. You deserve to make it. Here, have a look at this. " Daisy clicked the mouse to another site and typed in a password. A page displaying a card with the picture of a single pendant earring and Molly's name appeared. "I'm working on a business card for you. That earring with the amethyst on a white background would be nice. And we'll forget about the 'of New York' nonsense and just say Molly Creedon. What do you think?"

Molly stared at the screen. "It's stunning. I love it. But there are few things we have to take into consideration."

"Like what?"

"Like stock. At the moment, I have a lot of pieces from my workshop in Ireland. I was going to try to sell them at the market. But should they all be sold, I'll have a problem with production. I don't have a workshop here. If I do set one up, I'll need tools and material. I often use beaten silver and gold. Sometimes I use a method called the repoussé technique… it's when the metal is hammered on top of a particular kind of bowl. It requires special tools. And I wouldn't know where to get material. Gold and silver are expensive in France. I know where I could get the stones, though."

Daisy nodded. "I see. Well, I don't think it would be a problem for the moment. In any case, I don't see that you need to launch yourself into the mass market. Exclusivity is the way to go here. Make bespoke pieces for each customer. But let's get started and see what happens. We can order the business cards in any case. They only cost twenty euros for two hundred. That would be enough for now. Then I'll set up the website when we've agreed on a design. And I'll be displaying the jewellery whenever I go to a party. I already got some enquiries from women who liked the look of them."

Molly looked thoughtful. "How much would you charge for doing all this?"

"Nothing. Just the pleasure of wearing your jewellery."

"That doesn't feel right. Your work is so professional. I must pay you something."

Daisy thought for a moment. Normally this would have been a great opportunity to make some money. But Molly hadn't received any income from her designs apart from what she made selling her pieces at the market.

"If you insist. How about five percent of what you earn as the result of your new look?"

"Sounds like a good deal, sis," Liam said from the door of the kitchen. "I wouldn't look a gift horse in the gob, if I were you. And hey, why don't we make the old shed at the back of the garden your workshop? I'll get you the tools and workbenches or whatever the hell you need."

Molly laughed. "This is beginning to feel very much like a conspiracy. Okay. It's a deal."

Daisy spit into her hand and held it out. "Just like at the horse fairs in Ireland."

Molly spit into her own hand and shook Daisy's. "The deal is sealed."

Daisy laughed and wiped her hand on the back of her shorts. "Okay. Can I wash my hand now?"

Molly got up from the table and turned on the tap at the sink. "Here. We'll both have a good wash. Some horse dealers, huh?"

While they were drying their hands, Tommy raced into the kitchen. "Dayseee!" he shouted.

"Tommeee!" Daisy shouted back and held out her arms.

Tommy ran across the floor into Daisy's arms and hugged her with all his might.

"Hi! I'm back!"

Daisy put her cheek to his warm hair, which smelt of grass and sunshine.

"So I see. I missed you. Did you have fun in Ireland?"

Tommy looked up at Daisy. "Yes. We stayed at a farm and I got to feed the lambs that didn't have a mammy and I milked the cows and rode on a pony. And I lost a tooth, see?" He lifted his chin and opened his mouth for Daisy to see the gap. "The tooth fairy left two euros under my pillow. I bought some gobstoppers but they didn't work, Auntie Molly said. They didn't stop my gob at all."

"What's a gobstopper?"

"A kind of sweet," Molly said. "Or candy, as you say in the US."

"Why do you call it candy?" Tommy wanted to know.

Daisy shrugged. "No idea. Lots of words are different from British and Irish English in the US."

"Why?" Tommy asked.

"I don't know. I guess it's because some words that were used in old English still remained in the US when you changed them around over here. And then there are lots of people in the US from other countries and they used their own words, and then they were blended into American English."

"Oh." Tommy looked as if he had lost interest. "Okay," he said and wriggled out of Daisy's arms. "I have to go and wake Asta up. She's awfully sleepy when it's hot."

"So would I be if I were covered in fur," Daisy said. "Must be very hot."

Tommy laughed. "You'd look funny covered in fur."

"I don't know," Liam drawled from the door, where he had been watching them. "I think she'd look cute. Nice to cuddle up to on a winter's day."

"Ha ha," Daisy said, feeling her face flush.

Liam winked. "Anyway, I have to get to work if I'm to meet the deadline." He walked through the kitchen but stopped at the door. "Molly, this guy's coming to give us a quote for the alarm system. Give me a shout when he's here. He said around two o'clock."

"Alarm system?" Daisy said to Molly when Liam had left and Tommy had skipped into the garden in search of Asta.

Molly glanced out through the open door and lowered her voice. "Yes, we have to have one installed. We meant to do it earlier but never got around to it. But now, with all the burglaries in the area…"

Daisy stared at her. "Burglaries? I haven't heard anything about that. But then I have been very lazy about catching up with the news."

"There have been a number of break-ins and hold-ups in this area—more than usual. It's as if there is an influx of criminals right now, the police said. Our neighbours in the pretty villa next door were the latest victims. Two masked men broke in in the middle of the night and locked the whole family in the bathroom while they raided the house." Molly shuddered. "Awful."

"Gee, I had no idea. That's pretty scary. I suppose there's no way of identifying them?"

"No, other than they spoke with foreign accents." Molly shrugged. "Not a lot to go on. There are so many foreigners around here, including us. If they were to arrest everyone who speaks bad French, we'd all be in jail."

"I'd get life for not speaking it at all," Daisy joked. "Thank God I have an Irish passport…thanks to my granny being born in Ireland. An EU passport is better than a US one in France."

"Probably. But in any case," Molly continued, "we have to have a good security system now that I'm raising my profile as a jewellery designer. A safe isn't enough. And I'd hate to have someone break in and frighten Tommy. He's had enough traumas in his young life."

Daisy stirred her coffee and looked at Molly. "Traumas? You mean losing his mother? But he was very young, wasn't he? He'd hardly remember that."

"He was two. I don't think he remembers much about his

mother. But his dad's grief was horrible to watch. And it lasted a long time. He had these fits of temper and long drinking sessions. That's when I stepped in and started looking after Tommy. I made Liam see a therapist. He needed to deal with that anger. He's much better now, I'm happy to say."

"How did is wife die?"

"Cancer. She wasn't ill very long. About a year. She was only twenty-six when she died. So tragic. They were so happy."

"What was she like?" Daisy asked, even though she knew she should let go of the subject. It seemed to make Molly sad to talk about it.

"She was beautiful. Blonde. Sexy. She had this wicked sense of humour and a raunchy kind of laugh." Molly sighed and stared into the distance. "They were so in love. And when Tommy was born, they seemed like the perfect family. She was pregnant with their second child when cancer struck. The baby died, too. So it was a double tragedy in a way."

Daisy felt her eyes fill with tears. "That must have been unbearable for Liam."

Molly nodded. "Yes. It nearly broke him. But I think his writing saved him. He got lost in the stories he created, and it helped turn his mind away for limited periods."

"But what about you, Molly? Don't you want to have your own life, your own family? You've done so much for Liam. Isn't it time you thought about yourself?"

"Oh yes. But right now I'm trying to get established as a designer. I can do that and look after Tommy at the same time. Liam still needs my help. I love this part of France. I was in a relationship that didn't last. Probably my fault but it wasn't to be. So it suits me for now." She straightened her shoulders and smiled. "But things are looking up. Liam's better and he loves living in France. His career's on the up and that's another thing that helps him. There's only one thing missing."

"What's that?"

"A woman. He needs someone special in his life. I keep telling him to start dating. It's been long enough. And here, he's surrounded by beautiful women. But…"

"But?" Daisy echoed.

Molly sighed. "He'll never find a girl like Maureen. That's what he said only last night. I don't think he'll ever fall in love again."

* * *

Daisy worked hard on the website design into the late evening, only breaking for dinner with Irina on the terrace around eight o'clock.

Irina, looking tired, wolfed down her fillet steak and French fries.

"I'm very hungry," she said as if in reply to Daisy's stare. "So I asked the butler to make me some fries. I know I should have salad instead, like you, but I don't have to worry about getting fat anymore."

Daisy looked at Irina's trim figure and thought it would be a pity to ruin it. But maybe Irina needed a little comfort food?

"That must be a relief," she remarked.

Irina nodded. "Yes it is. A great relief." She stuffed the remaining fries into her mouth and took a swig of wine. "So, what was the party you went to like?"

Daisy cut into her steak. "It was quite nice. Beautiful house."

"The house outside Ramatuelle? Owned by Antonio… what was his name again?"

"Lorenzo."

Irina narrowed her eyes. "The Italian? The one who owns practically everything from Rome to Milan?"

"I think that's him."

"I've never been there. Nice house?"

"Lovely."

"I suppose there was a lot of security? I mean like alarms and electronic locks on the doors?"

Daisy thought for a moment. "No, don't think so. I mean, the usual. I saw some kind of control panel inside the front door when I went to the ladies."

Irina leaned forward, her fork in mid-air. "That was it?"

"As far as I could tell, yes. Strange, considering the beautiful paintings and artwork in the house. Must be worth a lot."

"How careless," Irina said and leaned back. "We have very good security in this house. But that's because we're from Russia."

"I suppose there's a lot of crime there."

"Yes," Irina agreed. "A lot of crime. And a lot of conspiracy. Everybody is watching everyone else." She shuddered. "Horrible."

"You must have been glad to leave and come here."

Irina nodded. "Yes. Very glad."

"Except you can't go out and about very much here."

"No, but I will one day. When I have a new passport."

Daisy laughed. "You mean if you find a man from around here to marry you?"

"Maybe. But there are other ways," Irina said cryptically. She put her elbows on the table. "So, tell me more about the party. Was it fun? Good food? Handsome men? Beautiful clothes?"

Daisy pushed away her plate. "Yes. All of that."

"You said..." Irina paused. "That there was a nice art collection in the house?"

"Yes. I saw at least two fabulous impressionist landscapes. And a little bronze horse I think was by Degas. That was just in the living room as I walked through." She suddenly giggled. "Antonio says he has a Picasso in the bedroom, but that's just a ploy to get girls into bed with him, I'm sure. He's so freakin' cheesy, it makes me laugh."

"Freakin'? Is that American?"

"I guess it is, yes."

"So you're an American citizen? I thought you were Irish."

Daisy picked up her glass of wine. "I'm both."

"Both?"

"Yes. I have two passports. American, because I was born there. And Irish because my granny was born in Ireland. And I needed an EU passport to work in Europe,"

"I see." Irina looked thoughtful. She quickly finished the pile of fries on her plate and got up. "I have to make a phone call."

"Okay. I have stuff to do, too. Then I think I'll go to bed. So I'll say goodnight."

Irina didn't reply. Without looking back, she walked away, across the terrace and into the house, like a woman on a mission.

Slightly puzzled, Daisy stayed on the terrace, finishing her rosé wine and looking at the bay infused with the rosy glow of the setting sun. This time of the evening was her favourite part of the day: when the sky slowly darkened, the wind dropped and the air was full of the sound of crickets and the cooing of doves. What a romantic setting. But here she was, all alone with no one to hold her hand or share her thoughts and feelings. She looked up at the sky and the new moon that was just rising and wondered if she was destined to spend the rest of her life alone.

Chapter 13

"I'm going to a spa for two days," Marianne said on the phone. "I get so tired talking to people, don't you? I need time to just chill. But I thought you might like to join me. It's just for two days. We could plan Molly's launch party at the same time."

"When?"

"I leave tomorrow. Lovely spa hotel not far from here. My treat, of course. What do you say?"

Daisy hesitated. She had just finished Molly's website, which had taken many hours of hard work. Molly and Liam were setting up the workshop, where Molly had decided to receive eventual clients who might want to put in orders. It was all going ahead as planned. But she didn't know if she could leave the house for two days. What about the dogs? And some of the furniture was yet to be delivered, including the dining table and chairs that had been delayed due to a strike in Italy.

"I'll have to call you back," she said to Marianne. She went to the downstairs office to find Irina, who, her hair wild and her face red, was typing furiously on the computer. Daisy knocked lightly on the open door. "Irina? Excuse me, but I need to ask you something."

Irina stopped typing and looked up. "Yes?"

"Uh, well, I have been invited to a spa hotel for two days. I'd love to go, but the dogs…"

Irina's eyes lit up. "You're going away? For two days?"

"Well, yes if…"

"What's the problem? Oh, the dogs. Don't worry about them. I'll get someone to walk them while you're away."

"You will? But…how?"

"I have an associate…I mean a friend, in town. Very reliable. He'll take the dogs for their long walks." Irina waved her hand at Daisy. "You go. Have a good time."

"Well, if you're sure."

"Of course I'm sure. The spa will be good for you. When are you going?"

"Tomorrow. I have that party tonight, and then I thought I might drive to the hotel in the morning."

Irina nodded. "Big party. You're wearing the jade set with the Chanel dress, yes?"

"That's right."

"Good." Irina turned back to the screen. "It's all fine. I'll help you with the make-up tonight and then you go to the hotel for the spa weekend tomorrow," she said in a tone that didn't allow arguing.

"Great. Thanks."

Irina nodded and picked up the phone. "Please close the door when you leave."

Daisy did as she was told, hearing Irina talking in rapid Russian into her phone as the door closed. Then she switched to English. Daisy was about to tiptoe away, but curiosity got the better of her. She pressed her ear to the door and listened to what Irina was saying. The conversation was brief and quite uninteresting. Daisy was about to walk away, but Irina's final words before she hung up made her freeze.

"Yes, I promise. The coast is clear for the whole weekend."

* * *

That night Daisy went to a cocktail party wearing a jade necklace and matching earrings, teamed with a cream, full-length, linen shift from Chanel. She had been practically mobbed by assorted women, all wanting to know where they could pick up such stunning costume jewellery. She had taken their contact details and said she would be in touch with an invitation to the launch and handed out Molly's business card with her website address. Liam, busy networking on his own, barely glanced at her. She had a feeling he was stepping away, trying to get some distance between them. He probably didn't really like her and had just flirted with her for a bit of fun. That hurt more than she wanted to admit. But better to back away and try to stay cool before she was in deeper and got hurt.

She walked around, talking to people about trivial things and listened to their conversations about their other homes, their yachts and problems with their servants. Gossip floated in the air, most of it quite nasty with comments about other people's love lives, cosmetic surgery and poor taste in decor. The men eyed the young women, who pretended not to notice. Except for coy glances, subtle smiles and winks, and the exchange of business cards, no one but the very sharp-eyed would have known anything at all was going on. But Daisy was very observant, her antennae twitching, picking up signals floating in the warm air. Because she was oddly detached from the inner circle of the rich, just floating on the surface, simply pretending she was one of them, she picked up some very strange and frightening vibes. In her designer clothes and the beautiful jewellery, she blended in seamlessly and nobody in this circle would ever have guessed her humble roots. And if they had done, they wouldn't have cared, as many of them came from very humble roots themselves. They didn't quite know who she was or what she did, except that they assumed she owned that modernistic villa on the hill and somehow had enough money to live like them. Daisy wondered what would happen if her cover was blown. She looked forward to the few days at the spa with Marianne, whom she found she liked more and more. She was so down to earth and friendly, never pretending for a moment she had been born to wealth. Marianne was also exceptionally nice to her servants, always asking them about their families and remembering their birthdays with little gifts. Daisy often heard some of the women talking about Marianne and how the people working for her never left.

"I tried to get her cook to work for me," one woman said, "but she refused to leave, even when I offered her more money." Daisy knew the reason—Marianne treated them like equals.

Standing by the window in the luxurious living room, Daisy sipped champagne and studied the elegant people talking to each other animatedly. Several people looked up and smiled, inviting her to join in. But she didn't feel like talking to any of them. She looked at the art collection on the walls and marvelled at the exquisite works by famous painters. It must be such a pleasure to have enough money to buy these works of art to display in a home.

"Incredible, aren't they?" a voice said by her side.

Daisy turned to Liam. "Yes. Amazing." She pointed at one of the paintings. Look, there's a little Van Gogh over there. One of his Arles paintings, I think. I love those the most, with that midnight-blue sky and the stars that look close enough to touch. That light really gets the feeling of a hot night in Provence, don't you think?"

He nodded. "Yes, you can nearly hear the soft sound of the crickets. They're so loud during the day, but at night they're more muted, barely audible."

"Do they ever sleep?"

"Probably not. I don't know much about insects to tell you the truth."

"Oh?" Daisy looked at him over the rim of her glass. "I thought you knew everything."

There was suddenly a serious look in his eyes. "Is that how I come across?"

Daisy decided to be honest. "Yes, sometimes. But maybe that's only when you talk to me. You can be very arrogant."

"You're awfully prickly. It might be that I respond to that. Maybe I'm trying to see the real Daisy? There's a lot more to you than a pretty dress and fancy hairdo, I feel."

She touched her hair that Irina had arranged in an elaborate French twist. "You don't like it?"

He looked at her in a way that made her blush. "It's fine. Very elegant." He moved closer. "But I prefer you with your hair down. Messy, eating sausages on my patio and laughing, with grease running down your chin. I wanted to kiss you then, grease and all."

Daisy took a step back and nearly dropped her glass. "Liam... I..."

"Don't tell me you don't feel the same. I can see it in your eyes." He took her glass, put it on the window ledge and grabbed her elbow. "Let's get out of here. Let's get to know each other better. Let's—well, you know what I mean." Looking deep into her eyes, he added, "Just say no and I'll leave you alone."

Unable to speak, her mouth dry with sudden desire, Daisy leaned against him, her knees wobbly. She knew then that she wanted him more than she had ever wanted any man. He was bad for her and it would probably end in tears, mostly hers. But at that moment she didn't care.

"Yes," she whispered.

He put his arm around her waist and pulled her close. "Yes...what? Yes, I should leave you alone...or you want to—"

"Shut up and get us out of here," Daisy mumbled in his ear. "I don't know where we're going to go, but just—"

His eyes dancing, he nodded and pulled her with him, waving to the people he knew, saying a brief goodbye and thank you to the hostess. Outside, while waiting for the valet to bring his car, he kissed her lightly on the lips. "This is torture."

"Where are we going?"

"My place."

"But Molly and Tommy?"

"Not there. Molly took Tommy to a friend's house in Saint-Maxime for the weekend. They have a pool and kids."

"You planned this all along."

"Did I? How clever of me."

"You scheming bastard."

"I love it when you talk dirty," he whispered in her ear.

"You ain't heard nothing yet," Daisy murmured.

"I can't wait."

The car arrived. They got in, kissed again and then Liam took off like a rocket. The car roared down the lane, through the quiet back streets of Saint-Tropez, out along the bay until it screeched to halt outside Liam's house. Her heart racing, Daisy looked at Liam. Did he feel what she felt? Was he as hot for her as she was for him? She lowered her gaze. She didn't want him to see the lust in her eyes.

He ran a finger down her cheek. "Last chance to back out. I'll still respect you if you say no."

She grabbed his hand and bit his finger. "Shut up. Let's get inside."

He pulled her close. "Yes, he whispered. I want to get inside *you*."

She started to laugh. "Geez, that's corny."

"I know, but you love it." He kissed her again, deep and hard and then let his mouth wander down her neck and into her cleavage, his lips hot on her skin. He fingered the heavy stones on the necklace. "This is like a suit of armour."

"I know. I have to take it off." Daisy finally managed to unravel her legs and open the door of the car. She got out and started walking toward the house. She heard the door of the car slam. Liam was beside her in an instant.

He took her arm. "It's a beautiful night. Let's go to the patio at the back."

They went around the house, through the archway onto the little patio illuminated by the moonlight. Liam pulled her to him again, and started to undo the clasp of the necklace, which he placed carefully on a nearby table. Then his hands went to the back of her dress and deftly undid every little hook all the way to the waist. He pulled at it, but Daisy stepped away and slipped out of it herself, the soft fabric skimming her hips, landing around her feet like a pool of cream silk. Stepping out of it, in only her bra and kickers, she felt a rush of air on her nipples from the light breeze through the thin silk of her bra. She could hear a rustle of fabric as Liam took off his clothes. Then he stood up and she could see the moonlight play on his toned torso and flat stomach. Oh God, he was hot. Sexy with a rough edge.

The dark shadow of his erection made her breath quicken. She was going to take off her bra and slide her knickers down her hips, but he was faster, stripping her in seconds until they were both naked. Then his body pressed against her, and she could feel his hairy chest against her breasts and his breath on her face, his hands on her buttocks and his erection pressing against her groin. They didn't speak, their quick breathing and quiet moans the only sound in the still warm night.

Two sun loungers stood side by side behind the oleander hedge, and Liam pulled Daisy down on one of them. She found herself surrendering to his touch, to the feel of him, the clean scent of his body and his tongue probing her mouth. He cupped her buttocks and pulled her even closer. Then he pushed hard inside her and they started to move together, finding the perfect rhythm, the perfect way to reach a climax that rocked their bodies and blew their minds.

When they were finally still, Daisy breathed out. "Oh, my Lord," she whispered.

Liam rolled off her. "Darlin', after sex, you don't have to stand on ceremony and call me My Lord."

Daisy giggled. "You were more than that."

He took her hand. "You're amazing. We were amazing."

"We were," she whispered, and smiled into the darkness. "Oh God, I'm still hot. I need to cool down or I'll explode."

"Shower?" he asked. "Or swim? The beach is only a step away. And it will be deserted. What do you say?"

"A swim sounds like heaven. But what if someone sees us? It's a public beach."

"There are towels on the other lounger. We can cover up with them until we get to the water."

Daisy got up and found a towel. Wrapping it around her, she walked the short distance to the beach, across the sand until she reached the water's edge. She dropped the towel and waded in, the waves lapping her legs. She could hear Liam behind her. He caught up with her and together they threw themselves into the cool water. Daisy swam a few strokes and then floated on her back, looking up at the stars, Liam beside her.

"Strange," he said. "Floating here with you, I feel a sense of infinity. And a connection with someone I lost. She's up there, you know, among the stars. Waiting for me."

"Like all the people we loved and who left this earth," Daisy said, looking up at the vast expanse of the Milky Way.

"It's so silent, so huge. And very frightening."

"Makes me feel smaller than a speck of dust."

Liam was silent for a while, just moving his arms slowly to keep afloat. "You lost someone too?"

"Yes. My dad. When I was twelve. Twenty years ago. Long time, but—"

"It never goes away, does it?"

"No."

He took her hand under the water. "I'm sorry. That must

have been hard. I often worry about Tommy. He lost his mother when he was only two. How's that going to affect the rest of his life?"

"I'm sure he'll be fine," Daisy said softly. "He has a dad who loves him. And his Auntie Molly too."

"He won't remember his mother."

"Maybe he will in a way? Maybe, deep in his heart, he has a memory of being held and loved by his mother. And if you tell him about her and keep her memory alive, he'll get to know her in a different way."

Liam let go of her hand. "Yes. You're right. I should tell him more about Maureen and how much she loved him. And how sweet and brave she was. How truly loving and kind. If we talk about her, she'll always be with us. That's a very comforting thought. Thank you."

"I'm glad if I could help in some small way." Suddenly feeling as if a third person had invaded her space, Daisy turned onto her stomach and started to swim back to shore. "I'm getting cold."

Liam kicked his legs in a slow backstroke. "Yes. I'd better get you home."

Daisy knew then that the spell was broken and that the sex had only been an interlude that meant very little to him. His mind and his heart were still so full of his love for his dead wife, he would never let go of her memory. The knowledge made her whole body feel heavy with pain and sadness. He would never look at her with anything other than lust.

They were quiet during the trip to the villa. When they arrived, Liam held the door of the car open for Daisy as she got out. Then he pulled her close and kissed her cheek.

"Thank you for a magical evening. And thank you for understanding." He tucked a strand of her hair behind her ear. "You're so lovely. You deserve someone a lot better than me."

She caught his hand. "No, you're wrong. I—" She stopped, knowing that nothing she said would change anything. He could never love anyone like that again. And they both knew it.

Chapter 14

"Ooohhh…" Marianne moaned. "That is sooo goood. You simply can't beat a good massage."

On the table beside her, Daisy closed her eyes and gave herself up to the skilled hands of the pretty Asian woman kneading her shoulders. "It's the best massage I've ever had."

"This is my favourite spa in the whole world," Marianne mumbled, lying on her stomach with her face in the hole of the massage table. "A bit lower down, please. Yes, that's it. Just below my shoulder blade. A very tight spot."

They were in the Château de la Messardière near Tahiti beach, an exclusive spa hotel, where Marianne had taken a suite for two days to have what she called 'the works', which meant facials, steam room, sauna, more facials, full body exfoliation, body wrap and massage. The evenings were spent doing yoga and eating detoxing food, followed by meditation. It made her feel ten years younger and gave her a break from the stress of entertaining and going to parties, she told Daisy.

"So that's your secret?" Daisy said that evening, looking at Marianne's fresh-faced beauty over a quinoa and beansprout salad on the hotel terrace overlooking the garden with its turquoise pool, the vineyards beyond and the intensely blue Mediterranean in the distance.

Marianne drank some water. "That and good genes. My mother's in her seventies but still very beautiful. Lovely skin.

But then her generation didn't roast in the sun like we did." She studied Daisy. "You look pretty good yourself. You have that sallow skin that never burns. Is that from your Italian side?"

"Must be. My mother still looks pretty good. She's only in her early sixties—not as old as yours, but she had a tough life."

"In what way?"

"She became a widow before she was forty."

"Your dad died?"

Daisy nodded. "I was twelve."

"I'm so sorry," Marianne said with deep sympathy. She touched Daisy's hand. "How awful to lose your father at that age. Mine died only a few years ago. But he was nearly ninety and very ill. His death was a relief to us all. Sad, of course, but not a tragedy. I miss him but I'm happy to think he's in a better place." She gestured to the sky with her fork. "Up there, I mean. In the next life. I believe there is one, you know."

"Me too."

Marianne looked relieved. "Oh, that's good. I'm glad. Not many people do these days. Nobody seems to talk about it. I mean, to say you're a Christian and believe in God is more shocking than sharing details of your sex life in my circles. It makes people feel uncomfortable. And all this dieting, fitness, yoga and plastic surgery makes them think death is somehow *optional*."

Daisy laughed. "I know what you mean. And living a long life is more important than living a good one."

"Exactly." Marianne speared a cherry tomato with her fork. "How did your mother cope when your dad died? He must also have been very young."

"Yes. He was thirty-eight. She was thirty-five. How did she cope? She did in her own way. Better than I did."

"You were twelve, for God's sake. How could you possibly compare?"

"I guess that's true. I was so mad at him for dying, you know? That was the hardest part."

"But he left all that money, didn't he?" Marianne said.

"Well…" Daisy looked down on her plate, then out across the expanse of gardens, vineyards and sea. What a beautiful setting. And what a nice woman Marianne was. So warm and genuine. It didn't seem right to sit there and lie to her. It was time to come clean. She took a deep breath. With butterflies in her stomach and her hands clammy, Daisy leaned forward and looked into Marianne's kind blue eyes.

"Marianne, I have something to tell you. Please don't hate me after this."

Marianne looked alarmed. "What? You're having an affair with Klaus? That's the only reason I could hate you."

Daisy let out a laugh. "No, of course not!"

"What is it then? You're gay? Or you're really a man and you fancy me?"

"I do fancy you. But not as a man. It's more like a girl crush. But please, just listen."

"Okay." Marianne sat back. "I'm listening."

"I'm not rich," Daisy said. "My dad didn't leave me any money. In fact, I'm poor. As in stony broke without a job. Well, I do have a job of sorts, but that'll end very soon, and then I don't know what I'm going to do."

Marianne stared at her. "You're poor? But what about the villa, the clothes, the jewellery? And that fancy car you drive?"

"All borrowed."

Marianne looked confused. "Borrowed? How do you mean?"

"I was hired as a house-sitter for the villa. The owners were away, I was told. They had these dogs they had to leave behind and the villa was just being set up, so my job is to oversee that and look after the dogs."

"Oookaaay," Marianne said, still looking bewildered.

"But what about all those designer dresses? And that haute-couture number you wore last night?"

"Borrowed as well. I got bored one night and started snooping around the house looking into every room. I wasn't supposed to but…"

"But you did anyway," Marianne filled in, looking excited. "Who wouldn't? That's what I would have done."

"Exactly. Then I found the master bedroom and the walk-in wardrobe packed with these clothes. All in my size, which was weird. So I—"

"Tried them on, of course!" Marianne squealed.

"Yes. And nearly at that same time, those invitations started to arrive. So…I decided to have a go, put on one of those dresses and see if I could blend in. At just about the same time, I met Molly, and she showed me the beautiful jewellery. I bought one of the necklaces and put it all on and went to the first party that happened to be yours and—" Daisy drew breath and sat back. "Well, that started the ball rolling."

Marianne laughed. "Like Goldilocks. What'll you do when the three bears arrive back home?"

"Mommy Bear already has." Daisy clapped a hand to her mouth. "Oops. I'm not supposed to talk about that."

Marianne's eyes lit up. "What? Who arrived back? I sense a mystery. You have to tell me."

Daisy squirmed. "I can't. Not right now anyway." She looked around the terrace that was becoming increasingly busy, with guests occupying nearly every table. Even though they were far apart, the earlier feeling of privacy was gone. She leaned forward. "I'll tell you later. If you promise not to tell a soul."

Marianne drew a finger across her heart and made as if to zip her mouth. "I swear. Cross my heart and hope to die. And you can believe that. When a Swede swears not to tell, it's like a sacred Viking promise. She'll take it with her to her grave."

Daisy laughed. "That sounds reassuring."

"It's the Viking way." Marianne looked around. "Too many people here. Let's go somewhere private. Like the balcony of our suite. We can have a glass of wine." She winked. "Strictly speaking, we're not allowed any alcohol on this detox diet. But one glass won't do any harm. And even if it does," she added, "who gives a shit?"

"Not me. I only came for the company and the massage."

"I just wanted to get away for a bit." Marianne confessed. "I don't really buy all that stuff about detoxing. I love the pampering, though."

"Me too."

"I want to hear the story of your life," Marianne declared. "I bet it's more interesting than mine."

Daisy laughed. "Are you kidding? You married a billionaire. What could possibly be more interesting than that?"

Marianne rolled her eyes. "It's not all it's cracked up to be, you know. If you knew what goes on under the surface of all this glitz and glamour…"

"Can't wait to hear it."

Marianne got up. "Not here." She winked. "Let's go to our suite and relax with a cup of herbal tea."

"And some of those yummy, sugar-free, quinoa cookies with fat-free butter."

Marianne smirked. "You got it. Let's go."

* * *

A while later, they sat on their own balcony, high above the garden with its pool and palm trees swaying in the light breeze, the sun dipping behind the mountains in the west. A wine cooler with a bottle of Rosé de St Croix sat on the table beside a plate with a runny Brie and a basket of fresh bread.

"This is cheating," Daisy said as she spread a lump of cheese on a piece of bread.

"Of course. But I always do." Marianne poured herself some wine. "Besides, cheese is good for you. Look at the majority of French women. All thin. And they eat loads of cheese and drink wine every day."

"Hmm, true," Daisy had to admit.

"So tell me about the mystery woman at your house."

"Not my house," Daisy protested. "Hers. Irina's. She's the wife of the owner. They're Russian. She snuck into France after a long drive from Moscow across Eastern Europe to Switzerland. Her husband has just divorced her and gave her the villa."

"Oh. That's intriguing. So I suppose she has to hide there until she sorts out her residency?"

"Exactly. In the meantime, she lets me wear her clothes."

"That's very generous."

"Not really. She doesn't like them. They were bought for her by her husband's assistant. He wanted her to look classy. Which, I might add, would be a huge challenge. She looks like a Turkish hooker and she likes it that way."

"Weird," Marianne remarked.

Daisy swallowed her mouthful. "Really weird. If you met her, you'd see what I mean. I don't trust her. I'm beginning to think she's planning something and wants me out of the way."

"Really? What?"

Daisy shrugged. "No idea. She seems to be making a lot of phone calls and sends e-mails all the time."

Marianne eyes widened. "Oooh, she's a spy! You'll have to keep an eye on her."

Daisy giggled at the thought of Irina spying for Russia. "I will. Then I'll call in the CIA when I find out what she's up to."

"Good idea." Marianne sat back on the lounger with her glass. "So, come on. Story of your life. Dish."

"Nooo," Daisy moaned. I want to hear the stuff about the underbelly of the rich."

"Your story first, then I'll share all that."

"Gee, you drive a hard bargain." Daisy sighed and sat back. "Okay. To make it short and snappy, I was the only child of an Irish-Italian immigrant couple. My dad worked in the construction industry, like many Irishmen. He was foreman on a big building site in Manhattan when he died in an accident. A crane broke and fell on his truck. He was killed instantly. I was twelve, nearly thirteen."

Marianne took Daisy's hand. "How awful."

"Yes it was. Especially for my mom. Not only was she devastated by the death, she then had no means of support. Except for sewing and making clothes for some of the neighbours, she hadn't worked much when I grew up. She wanted to stay at home for me, so I'd always have a parent there when I came home from school. It's the Italian way, you know."

Marianne nodded. "Very traditional. And good for the children. How did you cope? You said you didn't, but you were so young."

Daisy shrugged. "I thought I'd stay cool at school and not show how sad I was, how it had destroyed me to lose my dad. I managed to keep it together for a while. Nobody knew how hurt and lost and angry I felt. They all said I was so brave." Daisy let out a bitter laugh. "After six months of acting cool, I had some kind of breakdown. Couldn't stop crying for days and days. Couldn't eat or sleep or even talk. The school got me a therapist who helped me through the worst of it."

"Oh good. That must have helped."

"It did. It was good to talk to someone. But it must have been worse for my mom. She had no money and had to find a job. She tried to stay in the little house we rented. But then we had to move when she got a job as maid in a hotel in Manhattan. We shared a room there in the staff quarters, until I finished high school and had gone through a secretarial course. I moved out to share an apartment with four other girls in a flea pit in the East Village. Trendy now, but it sure wasn't then. Then I had a series of relationships with abusive men, one of whom brought me to France. I was more in love with France than with him, which he couldn't take, so we broke up. Then I got a job in a real estate agency and hooked up with yet another bastard who ended up evicting me from the apartment I was renting from his grandparents. When I saw the ad for the house-sitter job, I thought it was a perfect opportunity to leave town. So here I am, pretending to be one of you." Daisy drew breath. "Not very exciting, right?"

"Wrong. A bit too exciting, in a sad way," Marianne said. "What about your mother? Where is she now?"

"She moved to Vermont. A friend of hers is running a guest house there, so my mother joined up with her and they run it together. I think she's quite happy there. She's been dating this Italian-American for years. Nice guy. I think they'll eventually get married. Hope so, anyway. I'd like to see her settled. She's had better luck in love than me, that's for sure."

"Your history with men is awful," Marianne remarked. "Why do you go for guys like that? I bet Liam Creedon is no exception."

Daisy thought for a moment. "Why do I go for those men? No idea. Nothing to do with my dad, that's for sure. He was the sweetest, kindest man who ever walked this earth. And I miss him so much. But the guys I go for are mostly the bad boys. Don't know why. Could the challenge of taming a wild animal."

Marianne looked thoughtful. "I have always found men who ooze confidence very sexy. Maybe that's what attracts you them? Their confidence?"

"Could be," Daisy said. But she knew Marianne had put her finger on it. It was the confident men that made weak at the knees. "It's always the same story. It's fun to pitch your wit against them. I love a racy repartee. Then I fall for them and them for me. It's all fun and sexy until…until I start showing signs of wanting more, wanting a commitment of some kind. That usually puts the first nail into the coffin of the relationship."

Marianne nodded. "I think I know what you mean. Maybe that's my problem with Klaus? He's too sure of me. Takes me for granted."

"Maybe you should show more independence?" Daisy suggested. "Get into something he's not involved with. Make friends for yourself. Flirt a little with someone else? Make him worry a bit. You're beautiful and still young. Why not show you'd have the guts to go off without him?"

Marianne looked at Daisy with great appreciation. "You know, that's not a bad idea. Not all of it. But I might consider some of what you just said." A slow, wicked smile hovered on her lips. "It'll be fun to see how he reacts."

"Yeah, I'm looking forward to seeing a dent in that correct, perfect surface," Daisy agreed.

"What about you?" Marianne asked. "And Liam?"

Daisy blushed and looked away, the night with Liam still fresh in her mind. And his words before they parted.

"Him…oh, he…we…" she stammered. "Let's say it's complicated. And let's also say it's going nowhere, which might be a good thing."

"Probably not meant to be." Marianne poured wine into a glass and handed it to Daisy. "Here, have a glass of rosé. Then let's just chill for a bit. I'll put on a nice soothing CD.

They sat in silence, sipping wine and watching the sunset, listening to Acker Bilk play Stranger on the Shore. Daisy's mind drifted, going back to the night with Liam. He had been so sad when they talked about their lost loved ones. But somehow, she had given him comfort when she told him to tell Tommy about his mother in order keep her memory alive. But it had brought his wife closer to him, which meant he couldn't feel anything for anyone else.

Still so caught up in his grief, Daisy thought. *How can I compete with a dead woman?*

It wasn't possible. It hurt a little less than if he had rejected her, but it still meant they couldn't have any kind of relationship. What a shame, now that she was beginning to see and truly like the real man behind the tough façade. He wasn't like the men she normally fell for. He was more than that, better than that. Daisy sighed and blinked away her tears, trying to think of something more cheerful.

Daisy jumped when Marianne broke the silence. "I just had a wonderful idea for our last night here."

Daisy woke up from her daydream. "What?"

"How about dinner with two dishy men?"

"Which dishy men?"

"My husband and a surprise guest."

Daisy frowned. "You're not setting me up with someone, are you?"

"Not exactly. But there's this great guy who's just arrived in Saint-Tropez. He's a kind of cousin. He phoned to say he's moored his little sailing boat at the new harbour and will be spending a few days here before he sails off to The Balearics. I want to see him before he goes. He's always great company. I think you two would hit it off. Just for the evening, you know?"

"Is he confident?"

"Hmm." Marianne thought for a moment. "I wouldn't describe him as confident. More like self-contained. Calm. But great company. I think you'd like him. How about it?"

Daisy relaxed. "Why not? Could be fun."

Marianne unravelled her legs and got up from the lounger. "Wonderful. I'll go and call Klaus. They're going to have a South American band here tomorrow, too. We can eat, drink and dance under the stars."

"What fun." Daisy began to feel excited at the prospect. Meeting someone new might be just what the doctor ordered. And if he was related to Marianne, he had to be pretty special. Maybe her luck was turning? Maybe this was a new beginning?

* * *

"No need to dress up," Marianne declared the following evening, when they were back in their suite after the final programme of exercise, massage and top-to-toe beauty treatments.

"What do I wear then?" Daisy asked, flicking through the few items of clothing she had brought for the weekend. "I only have the yoga clothes, the shorts and T-shirt I came in, and the white linen pants and blue top I wore last night."

"Wear that then," Marianne said. "I'm just going in my pink silk shirt and the white cotton skirt from last night."

"But… I mean…"

Marianne smiled at Daisy. "You don't need to put on a show. Klaus will be in jeans and polo shirt and our guest will probably wear something similar."

"Our guest. I wish you'd tell me his name."

"I'm not going to say anything . I want you to make up your own mind when you meet him."

"Spoilsport."

Marianne walked to the door of her bedroom. "We have to get moving if we're to be down there at eight o'clock. Klaus doesn't like waiting. He's ordered champagne and hors d'oeuvres on the terrace, and then we move into the dining room for dinner." She looked at her watch. "We have twenty minutes to get ready."

Marianne disappeared into her bedroom and Daisy got ready. After a quick shower, she sprayed on some perfume and slipped into the wide, white, linen pants and the light-blue, sleeveless, silk top. The blue sandals she had bought in Saint-Tropez completed the outfit. Simple, casual and chic. Perfect for meeting a new man. Brushing her hair in front of the full-length mirror in her bedroom, she couldn't help noticing how her skin glowed and her eyes sparkled. The two days at the spa had done wonders, making her feel rested and calm after the upset with Liam.

Forget him, she told herself. *He isn't worth your tears.* She stuck out her chin and straightened her shoulders. No man was worth the kind of misery she had been through. From now on, she would call the shots. *Bring it on*, she thought. *Whatever this mystery man is like, I'll deal with him. He might be attractive, but probably not my type.*

Right on both counts, she realised only minutes later when, arriving at their table on the terrace, they were greeted by Klaus and the mystery guest. The two men rose when the women approached. The tall man beside Klaus held out his hand and their eyes met. Her heart stopped.

Chapter 15

They stared at each other. Daisy was the first to regain her powers of speech. "Oh my God—Ross?"

Ross took a step forward. "Daisy," he stammered. Where have you been? Why are you here with Marianne and Klaus?" Looking slightly dizzy, he kissed her on the cheek. "I looked for you everywhere after you ran off."

"I left a note. Thought you'd understand."

"I got the note," Ross said, still holding on to her hand. "But I didn't understand why you left like that. Or," he added sadly, "maybe I just didn't want to understand. You look amazing," he added.

Daisy pulled her hand out of his tight grip. "Thank you."

Marianne and Klaus stared at them. "You know each other?" Marianne asked.

"Yes," Daisy said. "We do. Long story. But...but..." Still shocked and confused, she looked at Marianne. "You said he was your cousin? How's that possible? I was expecting to meet a Swede, not a Canadian."

Klaus pulled out a chair. "Let's sit down and we'll explain. And by the way, good evening Daisy," he added with a little bow. "All the excitement made me forget my manners."

Marianne patted his cheek. "And why not, for a change? Let's be wild and irresponsible tonight."

Klaus looked at her with concern. "You haven't been drinking, liebling?"

Marianne sank down on a chair. "Not yet, sweetie. But I see the champagne arriving, so we'll soon remedy that situation. Right, Daisy?"

"Absolutely." Daisy made a thumbs-up sign and sat down on the chair Ross pulled out for her. "You're on, pardner."

The waiter served them each a brimming glass and set the bottle back in the ice bucket. The hors d'oeuvres arrived, and they were soon nibbling and talking, Marianne doing most of the nibbling and Daisy taking care of the talking.

"You have to explain why Marianne called you cousin, Ross. You couldn't possibly be real cousins."

Marianne swallowed her mouthful. "No, we're not. But my cousin was married to Ross' dad, when Ross was still Joseph-whatever, the heir to all those billions. And I spent a couple of months in the Bahamas with them when Ross was about—." She stopped. "How old were you, Joe, I mean Ross?"

"Sixteen," Ross said. "Not the happiest time of my life, I have to say. But you were a great help, darling cuz."

"I'm glad," Marianne said and looked at Ross with great fondness. "I wasn't very happy myself. But then, just after that, I met Klaus and we got married. And you ran away and became Ross." She studied him for a moment. "Must say you look much happier now. Much more mature and kind of settled in your head."

He nodded and topped up Daisy's glass, then his own. "That's true. I've managed to escape the jet-set world. The press isn't really interested in me anymore, so I don't have to hide. There aren't any scandals attached to my name...no sex, drugs and rock 'n' roll like with my dad. I'm just boringly normal and content doing my own thing."

"And you're off on a sailing trip?" Klaus asked.

Ross spread caviar on a cracker and handed it to Daisy. "Yes. I love sailing and windsurfing. And now it's still early summer and the winds and weather very favourable, so I thought I'd take a trip around The Balearics for a week or two. It was meant to heal a broken heart." He glanced at Daisy.

Daisy looked away. It felt like the cracker was going to choke her. This was embarrassing. Why did Ross have to say such a thing in front of other people? She squirmed as she met Marianne's probing eyes.

"It's a long story," she said, trying to convey she didn't want to discuss it.

Ross put his hand on her arm. "I'm sorry. It's a private matter, really. Let's just enjoy the evening and have fun."

Daisy relaxed. "Good idea. I can hear the band starting up. And the smell of the food from the dining room is making me very hungry."

Klaus got up. "Let's go to your table. I've already ordered for us all. Lobster salad, followed by sole meunière as that was what they recommended. I hope that's all right."

"Sounds perfect." Marianne beamed. "But I want crème brûlée for dessert."

"That's been ordered, too," Klaus said and put his arm around her. "You seem a little rebellious tonight, my darling."

Marianne wiggled her hips. "It's the music. Makes me want to break out and do something wild."

She meant it. Halfway through the meal, as the music got louder and more sensual, Marianne got up, grabbed Ross and said, "Come on, cuz, let's show them a few moves."

Ross didn't have to be urged. He jumped up and followed Marianne onto the dance floor, where they started to dance to the salsa music, as if they had both been born in Cuba. Daisy looked on in amazement as Ross changed from preppie boy to ballroom dancer. The sexy way he moved his hips and the hot looks he exchanged with Marianne as they danced a particularly slow, sensual Argentinian tango, her legs wrapped around his, their eyes locked, was a true star performance. The guests on the dance floor stopped dancing and cleared a space in the middle of the floor, while Ross and Marianne continued to dance as if they were hot for each other.

When the music ended, Ross bent over Marianne in a deep dip, their eyes still locked. Then they broke apart, laughing and bowing as everyone applauded. Marianne, her hair wild, her face flushed, ran to join Daisy and Klaus. She grabbed a glass of water before she sat down again, wiping her face on her napkin.

"Phew, that was hard work. But fun. Thanks, Ross. You were the best. Just like the old days, eh?"

"Yeah," Ross said, and regained his place beside Daisy. "But then I was a teenager. I could dance all night then, remember?"

"Yeah, me too. I was in my twenties. Being over forty knocks a bit of the edge off one's stamina, I have to say."

"You were incredible," Daisy said. "Where did you learn to dance Latin American like a pro?"

"In the Bahamas," Marianne replied. "There was a dance club on the beach with a Cuban band. We used to go there practically every evening to learn all the dances from this dance teacher. What was her name again?"

"Paquita," Ross said. "She was at least sixty years old and very fat. But boy, could she move."

"She used to call you snake hips," Marianne teased. "I think she had a crush on you."

Ross grinned. "Are you kidding? I had a huge crush on her. She might have been fat, but she moved like a cat. My first teenage love affair. Except for you, of course, cuz," he added and winked at Marianne.

She flicked a breadcrumb at him. "Oh, puhleeese. All the girls were mad about you. You were practically mobbed every time you went to the beach."

"They were after all that cash. Heirs to big fortunes are normally very popular with the girls. I'll never know if it was my newfound manliness or the size of my trust fund that was the biggest attraction." Ross sighed theatrically. "The hardships of being a rich young man know no bounds. Wouldn't you agree, Klaus?"

Klaus laughed. "I wouldn't know. I made my own money. When I was a teenager, I was always broke and I was awkward and spotty. Girls were like alien beings to me. I had no idea how to talk to them."

Marianne put her head on his shoulder. "But now you sure know how to make a woman happy."

"I'm glad to hear it," Ross said. "Because if you make her miserable, I'll come after you with a big stick."

Daisy looked at Ross as if she was seeing him for the first time. He was so different tonight—so confident and funny. It was a side she had never seen before. And the way he danced with Marianne had made her feel a slight pang of something. Jealousy? Sexual attraction? No, not possible. She didn't feel that way about him. Or did she? She kept looking at him, trying to find a clue to who he really was. He looked the same as ever, except his blond hair was a bit longer and his tan deeper. His blue-green eyes were, as always, the same colour as the sea on a sunny day, but there was a determined gleam in them as their eyes met.

The band started playing a slow samba. Ross took Daisy's hand and pulled her up from the table. "Let's dance and talk. Especially talk."

"Okay." She followed him onto the dance floor, where he put his arms around her and they started to move to the music, Daisy falling into the rhythm and Ross' expert dancing.

"I had no idea you could dance like this," she said.

He looked down at her, an earnest expression in his eyes. "There's a lot you don't know about me, Daisy."

She met his eyes. "Obviously." She pulled at his white Lacoste tennis shirt. "What else are you hiding behind that preppy facade?"

"Do you really want to know? Or are you just making polite conversation?"

She stopped dancing and detached herself from arms. Being so close to him no longer gave her the old comfort of being hugged by a brother. His hands on her waist and his breath on her hair made her feel very odd. This was different and slightly troubling. She didn't know how to react to him anymore. The old cosy feeling between them was gone. She suddenly felt it hard to breathe.

"Can we go outside?" she said. "It's getting a bit hot."

"You're telling me," he said with a laugh. "Let's go out on the terrace. Klaus and Marianne won't notice. They seem to be having a fight."

Daisy glanced in the direction of their table. Marianne and Klaus were indeed involved in some kind of argument, Marianne gesticulating and Klaus muttering something through clenched teeth. But Ross swept her out to the terrace which made her forget them.

Outside, they faced each other by the railing. "So," Ross said, "what have you been doing since you ran off?"

"I..." Daisy started. "I got a job as a house-sitter. I saw the ad in the local newspaper when you had gone back downtown. I replied to it by e-mail and got an immediate reply. Couldn't believe they'd give me the job on the spot like that."

"This was all done before I came back?"

"Yes," Daisy whispered.

"But you kissed me in a way that made me think—"

"I know." She hung her head and pressed her face against his chest. "I loved that kiss. But it didn't do what you might have hoped it would." She lifted her face and looked at him. "I'm very fond of you, Ross. But I didn't feel what you feel for me. I couldn't sleep with you on that basis. It would have been wrong. I know that's what you wanted, but I couldn't give you that. Not sleeping with you was harder than the alternative. It would have been nice, but also very wrong. That's why I ran away."

He pulled away and turned his back to her, staring out at the dark landscape. They were quiet for a long time, the only sound the faint rustle of the palm trees and Daisy's laboured breathing.

He turned to her. "Thank you for your honesty. Difficult to accept, but better than pretence, I suppose."

Daisy looked at him and wondered if it was possible her feelings for him had changed. The side of him he had revealed earlier was making him seem a lot more attractive. Maybe, if...

"Kiss me now," she whispered into the darkness. "I might feel differently."

He pulled her close, his lips hovering over hers. She closed her eyes, his hands on her shoulders and the feel of his body making her shiver. Then Liam's face popped into her mind and she stiffened, trying to push the image away.

Ross pulled away. "No. You're trying to force yourself to love me. I can feel it. It's not working. I don't want you to play with me. I don't want you to break my heart again."

"I wouldn't," she protested, suddenly cold with fear. "Ross, tonight, you showed a new side of you, a side I never knew existed. Meeting you again, dancing with you, I felt—" she stopped, feeling a wave of frustration and confusion wash over her.

"You felt—what?"

"Something different." She took his hand. "Not sure what it is yet."

He held her hand for a moment and then pulled it away. "You're still not sure, are you?"

"No, but—"

"That's not enough."

"What do you mean?" she exclaimed. "You've been flirting with me for over a year now. I always knew you were attracted to me. I didn't share those feelings, but we built up a friendship I treasure."

"So much so you ran off just like that?" he said bitterly.

Daisy put her hands on the railing and bowed her head. "It was a stupid thing to do, I admit." She turned to look at him. "But there were so many things going through my head, not least of all your money, I have to say."

"My money? Why should that be a problem?"

"Because I'm dirt poor. I don't think you could ever understand what that means, how it affects you. I have always been scratching for a living, always had to scrimp and save. Then I came here and was able to manage very well because I found a job I was good at. Not selling houses, but running the agency with Flora and setting up the website. So I was a little better off. Then I met you and discovered you're seriously wealthy but that the wealth had made you more miserable than happy. Of course, you fell in love with me and that became a problem."

"What kind of problem, for Chrissake?" Ross demanded. "You'd think it would have solved everything for you."

Daisy nodded. "It would have if I were the kind of woman who could fake fancying you right back. Who'd do anything for money. Who'd ruin a friendship forever and not worry about it. But I couldn't. I would have been living a lie. It would have ended in a lot of sadness."

"So what's the difference?" Ross asked. "The whole thing has ended anyway. And here we are, all sad and miserable."

"Has it ended? Really?" She grabbed him by the arm and moved up close to him, so close she could feel his breath on her face and smell the spicy aftershave he used. "I don't know what happened, but I—"

He took her hand off his arm and held it, covering it with his other one. "Daisy, this has made me feel confused and scared. I don't dare hope you're beginning to fall in love with me. I need to go away for a bit. To think and sort out my own feelings. I've been thinking about you for so long, hoping and wishing. You've been my number-one fantasy since the first time we met. I thought it was hopeless, but now you're telling me—" He paused. "I can't believe it's true. I can't trust you yet. Or me."

"What do you mean?" Daisy asked, bewildered. But then she began to think he was right. Maybe it was best Ross went off for a while. Liam and what had happened between them were still fresh in her mind. She needed to catch up with her own feelings about him, about Ross and everything. She pulled her hand away.

"Maybe you're right. I've thrown you a curve ball. I'm a little shaken myself, to be honest. So, go. Get going on your sailing trip. Then, when you come back we'll be calmer, more able to sort things out."

"Yes. I'll go." He seemed to hesitate for a moment, but it was too dark for Daisy to see his expression. Then he touched her lips with his in a light, barely there kiss. "I'll be back," he whispered. "Take care, Daisy." He stumbled away in the darkness, and she could hear him run down the steps and across the gravel in the garden below.

Chapter 16

"Men," Marianne said as they were having camomile tea in the living room of the suite before going to bed. "Aren't they hard work?" She looked beautiful but fragile, sitting there in her blue silk nightgown, her face clean of make-up and her hair brushed back.

Daisy sighed and stirred her tea. "Yeah. They sure are."

Marianne pulled her feet up under her in the sofa. "What's up with you and Ross? He left so suddenly after you had been out on the terrace for ages. I couldn't believe it when you said you knew each other. I just thought it would be nice for you two to meet, and then—wham—you looked as if you'd been punched in the stomach. And he went all white. So I realised there was some heavy stuff between you."

Daisy let out a hollow laugh. "Heavy? That's putting it mildly." She leaned forward in the deep easy chair and looked at Marianne. "It's not something I want to talk about, but since you were there, I'll give you the short version. I knew Ross when I was working in Antibes. Didn't know who he was at first—he was just some well-off guy who bought this beautiful house and was doing it up. We were both part of the windsurfing gang over there. We had a lot of fun and became close friends until—"

"Until he wanted more than friendship?" Marianne filled in. "And of course, being the nice sweet guy, he wasn't exactly your type?"

Daisy nodded. "You got it. And to add to it, I had just had that nasty break-up I told you about. Ross put me up at his place and said I could stay as long as I liked. But then I realised it would put his hopes up, so I left in a hurry, after an evening when he got a bit, uh, romantic. Couldn't sleep with him just like that when I didn't feel the way he did. I know a lot of women would, just for his money, but…"

"Of course you couldn't! Neither could I," Marianne said with feeling. "When I married Klaus, everyone thought I married him for his money. But that's not true. I fell in love with him the moment we met at that party in London. He swept me off my feet. I thought it was so romantic the way that stiff, correct German turned into a hot lover." She looked at Daisy with a dreamy expression. "Of course, his money was nice, and I so admired the way he had built up his own fortune by being smart and working hard. He wasn't born into money. He made it all himself. I'm very proud of him." She sighed. "But I feel we're drifting apart after all these years."

"How many years have you been married?"

"Twelve. He had just recovered after a nasty divorce from his second wife, a woman from Lithuania. She was like a lot of those women from Eastern Europe, whose only aim in life is to marry money. They're really scary. Many of them have degrees in economics. They go to London or Berlin or Paris and look up the names of hedge-fund managers and where they hang out…usually here in Saint-Tropez during the high season. These women, who are stunning by the way, just hang around in cafés and start flirting. Then they get invited to parties or on yachts and the show begins."

"The show?" Daisy asked, her eyes wide.

"Yeah. The sex. These girls do anything anywhere, all day and all night long. They're amazingly energetic and very accomplished. So the poor man doesn't have a chance. After a month or so of this, he's hooked. Then she pulls back and says, 'Oh, honey, I don't feel you love me enough, I don't feel you care enough about me to make a commitment.' So then of course come the proposal and the diamond ring and so on. Then she has one or two babies and kind of forgets about him. She won't really fit in with his classy friends, either, and the sex just peters out, too. And one day he wakes up and realises he married a Lithuanian hooker. So they divorce but—oops—they forgot the pre-nup during that first care-less rapture, so that split costs him mega bucks." Marianne drew breath, her eyes twinkling.

Daisy had to laugh. "Sad but kind of ridiculous in the end. I have a feeling that's exactly what's going on with Irina's husband. She told me he's fallen for some Czech woman with a degree in economics and sex. Is that what happened to Klaus?"

"Not really. He was smart enough to get her to sign a pre-nup. And there were no children. He has two daughters with his first wife, who's German. So when we met, he told me he didn't want children. I agreed, mainly because I had to have my ovaries removed after a cancer scare a year before we met, so I can't have a baby. But that doesn't make me sad at all. I don't think I'd make a good mother, anyway. And I love his daughters. They come for visits often and we have great fun. So I get to be a mum without the grief."

"That's lucky."

Marianne smiled. "Yes. I'm very lucky. I love my life with Klaus. But lately, as you know, I've been worried he might be looking elsewhere."

"I can't believe that."

"I could be wrong. He got wildly jealous tonight when I was dancing with Ross."

"You looked hot together," Daisy said. "And it was watching him dance and then joke around with you that made me see a new side of Ross. I started to feel differently."

Marianne nearly choked on her tea. "You mean you and he might…?" she said when she could breathe.

"No…I mean yes…maybe. We talked about it, but then he decided to go away for a while to think and to give me some space, too. We'll see what happens when he comes back"

"Love is in the air," Marianne chanted.

Daisy threw a cushion at her. "Shut up."

Marianne ducked, laughing. "And Liam?" she asked when she had recovered.

Daisy sighed. "That's another confusion. We're so attracted to each other, but I don't think we could have any kind of relationship. Even after—"

"After…what?" Marianne exclaimed. "What happened? You didn't—"

"Yes, I did. Oh God." Daisy put her hand over her face. "I shouldn't have had sex with him, but I couldn't help it. Big mistake."

Marianne sat up, her eyes on stalks. "What? You had sex with him? Really? Was it good?"

"Yes," Daisy mumbled. "Of course it was. But afterwards he said it had been some kind of mistake. Just a flash of physical attraction between us after drinking too much or something."

"He said that? What a shit."

"He's not a shit. He's just confused," Daisy countered. "He's still grieving for his wife, who died four years ago. He isn't over it yet. Maybe he never will be. I felt it that night."

Marianne peered at Daisy. "How did that make you feel?"

"I don't know. Really bad at the time. Thought I was sort of in love with him. I mean, who wouldn't be? But I can't compete with a dead woman." She looked at Marianne bleakly. "When I met Ross again, it threw me. When I was with Liam that night, I was so confused. I wanted to stay and run at the same time. I'm afraid to get on what I know will be a roller-coaster ride to hell. But with Ross, I'm so different."

"I've always believed that love is also about who you

become when you love someone. If that love brings out the good things in you, then it's real and true. But a lot of people confuse love with ownership. They fall in love and then they have to own that person. Men especially fall into this trap." Marianne sighed. "I want Klaus to be happy. If that means he'd be happier with someone else, then maybe I should accept it and let him go?"

Daisy put her teacup on the table. "Bullshit," she said hotly. "I think Klaus takes you for granted. You need to shake him out of that complacency."

Marianne's eyes were thoughtful. "You know what? I think you're right. I need to think about this and work out a plan."

"That's the right attitude." Daisy got up and stretched. "I have to go to bed. I'm exhausted. All this emotional stuff is draining. I need a good night's sleep so I can deal with everything in the morning. The house, that weird woman in the villa, and Molly and her launch. Not to mention Liam. I'm glad Ross left. I need time to sort myself out."

"Me too. Anyway, I need to get back home to look at our security system. Klaus told me Antonio's villa was broken into the other night."

"How awful."

"I know. Poor Antonio was devastated. Some of the best paintings stolen. Very clever heist. But his security system was outdated. Careless, but that's the Italians for you. Not very organised. He has to install a new system now, which won't be cheap. But of course he can afford it."

"I'm sure he can. Not very nice though." Daisy yawned. "Bedtime for me. I'm sure we'll have to look at our alarm system, too. Must mention this to Irina. Night, Marianne. Sleep well."

Marianne threw Daisy a kiss. "You too, sweetie. Time to get back to real life. Maybe we can both get our love lives back on track eventually. I'm going to shake Klaus up so he'll sit up and take notice."

"What are you going to do?"

There was a rebellious gleam in Marianne's eyes as she lifted her blond mane off her shoulders. "I have a plan…"

* * *

Daisy forgot about Marianne and her plan when she got back to the villa the next morning. Irina was nowhere to be seen and Olivier, busy with the vacuum cleaner in the living room, replied to her question with a shrug.

"The beach, maybe?" he shouted over the sound of the vacuum cleaner.

"And the dogs?" Daisy asked.

Olivier turned off the vacuum cleaner. "In their room. They were walked by a man earlier this morning."

"What man?"

Olivier shrugged. "A friend of Madame Irina. I think his name's Dimitri."

"Oh. The Greek?"

"They were speaking English."

Daisy stood there, thinking while Olivier turned the Hoover back on. Who was Dimitri? Irina had been talking to him on the phone. Was he her lover? Or…she was interrupted by the door opening, admitting Irina carrying two shopping bags.

"You're back."

"Yes." Irina, wearing a multi-coloured smock, white jeans and a straw hat, stepped into the hall while the door banged shut behind her. "I was careful, don't worry. But the gendarmes around here aren't checking the papers of people coming out of boutiques, you know. It's mostly poor and Arab-looking guys who get searched."

"That's a bit racist," Daisy remarked.

Irina put the shopping bags on the hall table. "Yes, it is.

But that's the way it is these days. All those terrorists, you know. And there have been a lot of break-ins, the girl in the shop said. Maybe the gendarmes think there is a link to terrorists groups?" She took off her hat. "Look, I had my hair done. You like?"

Daisy stared at Irina's new hairdo. Not only had she cut it to shoulder-length, but she had also had the colour changed to dark blonde with lighter highlights. Very similar to Daisy's own style and colour. "Yes, of course I like it. It's very like mine."

Irina touched her hair. "That's where I got the idea. This way we look more alike. You don't mind?"

Daisy couldn't decide if she minded or not. Even though Irina's new hairstyle was similar, they still didn't look alike. Irina's alabaster-white skin and hooded green eyes were a huge contrast to Daisy's golden complexion and large brown eyes. Although they were the same height and dress size, nobody could have mixed them up or think they were related in any way.

"Not at all," Daisy said after a long silence. "I'm quite flattered, really. But why do you want to look like me?"

"I find you very attractive. This way I look more European, instead of Russian." Irina hesitated. "I'm trying to get…someone to marry me once my divorce goes through. Someone with an EU passport."

"Dimitri?" Daisy asked.

Irina blinked and went suddenly very pale. "How you do you know his name?"

"I heard you talking on the phone with someone with that name. So I thought…"

"No, not him. Someone else," Irina said cryptically. She gathered up her bags. "I'm going into the office and I don't want to be disturbed."

"Of course." Daisy took her overnight bag and started up the stairs. "I'll just unpack this and then I'm going out."

"For how long?"

"No idea. I'll be back to walk the dogs, though."

"I will take care of the babies," Irina said. "You go and have a good time. No need to come back for dinner."

Daisy nodded. "Okay, thanks."

"You're welcome," Irina said and went into the office, banging the door shut. Daisy could hear her lock the door. Shaking her head, thinking how weird Irina was, she went upstairs to unpack, change into a fresh pair of trousers and a cotton shirt, and get ready to start work with Molly. She hoped Liam wouldn't be there. She didn't know how she could face him again. How would she be able to hide the strong attraction she felt or be able to even talk to him in a normal tone of voice? It seemed impossible. But maybe it was better to get it over with, than put it off? She nodded at her image in the mirror.

"Stay cool," she whispered. "Pretend you don't care."

* * *

Daisy didn't have to pretend anything. When she got to Liam and Molly's house, she found Tommy playing with Asta in the front garden. He rushed to the car when she pulled up.

"Hi Daisy! Asta can fetch the ball now. I taught her. Look. Catch, Asta!" He threw a tennis ball across the dusty lawn. Asta raced after it and picked it up. "Good girl," Tommy shouted and ran up to the dog, trying to prise the ball out of her mouth. But the dog growled and refused to give the ball back. Tommy looked at Daisy and sighed. "I can't get her to give it back, though."

"Try with two balls," Daisy suggested. "If you throw another ball, she'll let go of the first one and run after the other one."

Tommy looked impressed. "That's a great idea. I'll go and

get the other ball now from the kitchen. Hey, come with me. I think Molly wants to see you."

"Okay." Daisy hesitated. "Is your dad here?"

"No, he's gone into town to meet someone. They're going to talk business, he said, and it would be boring for me, so I had to stay here with Auntie Molly and Asta. But he said he'd be back for dinner, and then we're going to a place where they have great ice cream. Do you want to come?"

Daisy squirmed. "Uh, thanks, but I'm busy tonight. Maybe another time?"

"Okay." Tommy went around the house and into the kitchen, Daisy in tow.

Molly was at the kitchen table, working on her laptop. She looked up when they came in. "Hi, Daisy. You've no idea how happy I am to see you! You really started the ball rolling at that party last week." Molly pushed her hands through her wild curls, making them stand on end. "I got all these e-mails asking about making pieces for some women, and I don't quite know what to do." She turned the laptop so Daisy could see the screen. "I don't have enough stock and don't know if I can meet these orders. The workshop's nearly finished, but I'm still waiting for tools to arrive."

Daisy glanced at the screen. "They sure are keen. But don't worry, Molly, just reply to them all in the same e-mail and say they'll be very welcome to meet you at the launch of the new collection at the home of Mrs Marianne Schlossenburgh on July twelfth and you'll discuss it all with them then. Great that they're so interested, though."

"How do I send them all an e-mail without revealing everyone's e-mail address?"

"You send a blind copy. It's like sending a cc, but you go for bcc instead. Then nobody sees anyone else's mail."

Molly frowned at the screen. "Oh, I see. Thank you, Daisy. That's a huge help. I'm such a klutz when it comes to the Internet."

"You're welcome. How many e-mails did you get?"

"About twenty or so."

Daisy pulled out a chair and sat down beside Molly. "Awesome. That's another twenty guests for the launch. And Marianne's inviting at least fifty more. This is going very well. Have you enough pieces for Marianne and me to model at the launch?"

"Yes. Plenty. I brought some nearly finished pieces with me from Ireland. They'll be all done and polished in time. They're all in the workshop. Liam has had security locks installed there and I have a new safe. So, everything's in the same place. Do you want to see it?"

"I'd love to. Last time I was here, it was just an old shed."

"Liam's worked so hard to turn it into a proper workplace for me. He even took a break from writing for a couple of days to get it finished, even though he has a very close deadline."

"Yes," Tommy cut in, still rummaging in the toy box for a ball. "He works at night now to catch up. I heard him clicking on the computer in the middle of the night."

Molly sighed. "That makes me feel guilty. He shouldn't have worked so hard on it when he doesn't really have the time. But that's Liam for you. Always thinks of others first. " She turned off the computer and got up from the table. "Come on, I'll show you the new workshop." She led the way out of the kitchen and across the courtyard and up the incline to the little stone-faced building. Daisy glanced at the lounger beside the hedge with a shiver as they passed it. Had it really happened? Yes it had. She blushed as she remembered.

Molly opened the wooden door of the shed and stepped inside, Daisy and Tommy at her heels.

"Here it is," she said. "My little hideaway."

Daisy looked around in amazement. What appeared to be an old shed on the outside was a quaint but modern workshop inside. The floor had been laid with wide oak planks and the stone walls were covered with colourful Celtic tapestries. A work bench stood against the far wall, littered with polished stones of every size and hue, and tools of all kinds stood in neat rows in stands at the back. There was a tall lamp with a steel shade and a padded stool, the height of which could be adjusted according the position Molly needed when she worked. Beside it was a small desk for working on a laptop with a more comfortable office chair. There was a wicker seating arrangement under one of the windows through which mellow sunshine cast a soft light into the room. Classical music wafted from stereo speakers beside the workbench and a branch of jasmine in a blue jug filled the room with its sweet scent.

"What a wonderful space," Daisy said.

Molly sat down on one of the wicker chairs. "Yes, it's fabulous. Liam did a great job. He didn't do all the physical work himself. He got a contractor to lay the floor and found the workbench in an old factory. I picked the rest of the furniture and brought the wall hangings from Ireland."

Daisy joined Molly by the window. "I can see it'll be a very nice place to work in and to receive clients."

"And she can see me through the window when I play outside," Tommy said.

Molly ruffled his hair. "So I can."

"Why don't you get the laptop and we'll do the rest of the stuff in here?" Daisy suggested.

Molly nodded. "Good idea. But it's nearly dinner time. I put a chicken in the oven about an hour ago. I'll do a salad to go with it and get Liam to swing by the bakery for fresh bread on his way back. You'll stay and eat with us, won't you?"

"I already asked and she said no," Tommy cut in. "But maybe if we say pretty please?" He looked at Daisy and batted his eyelashes. "Pretty please, Daisy, have chicken dinner with us, will ya?"

Daisy laughed and ruffled his hair. "How can I resist such charm?" She realised it would be awkward to meet Liam again, but wasn't it better to have it over with? They would have to meet again and again if she was going to continue working with Molly. But she had to come clean and tell them who she really was. No more pretending to be wealthy. Butterflies danced in her stomach as she contemplated facing Liam. She looked at Molly and took a deep breath.

"Thank you. I'd love to stay for dinner."

Chapter 17

It wasn't as bad as she had feared. When Liam arrived, they had already started eating, seated at the round table in the courtyard. Daisy didn't know if it was the two glasses of rosé or Molly's friendly chatter interspersed with Tommy's musings or the cosy feeling of being, somehow, part of this family group that made her relax. But whatever it was, she was able to meet Liam's eyes and say hello without too much embarrassment. He did a double-take when he saw her, but immediately seemed to catch the vibes and greeted her with a smile that conveyed both warmth and a kind of apology.

Liam put a fresh baguette on the table, and Molly heaped a plate with roast chicken and salad and handed it to him. "You must be hungry."

"Starving," he said and fell on the food.

Molly cut up the baguette, put it all in a bread basket and handed it around.

Liam put his hand on Tommy's head. "Hey, partner, I haven't forgotten about the ice cream. We'll go as soon as I've finished my dinner."

Tommy's face brightened. "Yippee! Ice cream!" He grabbed a piece of bread and slid down from his chair. "I'll play with Asta while I wait. Can I go, Auntie Molly?"

"Yes, if you take your plate and bring it into the kitchen."

"Okay." Tommy took the plate and disappeared through the kitchen door.

"And don't let Asta lick the plate," Liam shouted after him. "Not that he listens to me," he said with a shrug. "Molly's the boss around here." He shot a crooked smile at Daisy. "So what have you been up to with my sister, princess?"

Daisy dropped her cutlery with a clatter onto her plate. "Me? Oh well, we've—" She stopped. Now was the moment to come clean. "We've been doing some work on the website and then worked out a plan for—" She stopped again. "Whatever. It's going well. But I have something to tell you both. Something important."

"This sounds ominous," Liam said and stuffed the last of his baguette into his mouth. He chewed and swallowed. "So, go on. Is this going to change life as we know it?"

"No, but it might change how you look at me. What you think of me, I mean." Her hands clammy and her mouth dry, Daisy looked at Molly. "I hope you won't hate me when I've told you."

"Hate you?" Molly asked, looking confused. "How could we hate you?"

"You're not going to tell us you're really a man and your name is Derek, are you? Or that you're a member of the CIA and have murdered several people? Or that—"

"Shut up, Liam," Molly snapped. "Let Daisy speak. Can't you see how nervous she is?"

"Okay," Liam said, looking at Daisy. "So speak."

"I'm not who you think I am," Daisy started. "I mean *what* I am, really."

"Depends who you think we think you are," Liam said and winked at her. "So spit it out, will ya? I haven't got all evening."

"Right, okay." Daisy cleared her throat. "I'm not the rich heiress I've been pretending to be. I'm just house-sitting that villa. I was just going to do my job and walk the dogs and then leave when the two months I was hired for were over. But then I found a whole wardrobe full of designer clothes and all these invitations came in. I just couldn't resist it. I was bored and lonely, so I started going to all those parties and telling all kinds of lies, just because I wanted to see how it felt to be rich."

"What?" Speechless, Molly stared at Daisy.

"So you're not a real princess?" Liam said after a long silence.

Daisy felt her face flush. "No. I'm not. I didn't go to fancy schools or grow up on Fifth Avenue. I grew up in Brooklyn and my mother was a maid." She drew breath.

Molly's eyes widened. "Holy Mary. It was all made up?"

Daisy nodded.

"Well, I'll be…" Liam said, looking stunned. "You sure put on quite a show, darlin'."

"Yes, I suppose I did," Daisy said with a deep sense of shame. She looked at Molly. "It was just a bit of fun. Until I met you. Then I realised I couldn't keep it up anymore. You're such a good friend. I couldn't go on lying."

Molly nodded. "I can see that. Gosh, must say this is a bit of a surprise." She leaned over the table and put her hand on Daisy's arm. "But don't worry. I truly understand. It was a kind of game that snowballed until you couldn't stop."

Daisy nodded. "Yes. Something like that."

We can still keep working together, can't we?" Molly asked.

"Of course," Daisy exclaimed. "More so now than before. I really want to help you get your business launched."

Molly started to laugh. "I'm sorry but it's kind of funny. I can see how it all happened. I think I would have been quite tempted to have a go at it myself. Not that I'd look as good as you in designer clothes."

Daisy turned to Liam. "I hope you won't think too badly of me after this."

He looked at her thoughtfully. "Badly? I'm not sure. But it changes things for me. Completely."

Daisy sighed. "I knew it would." She pushed her plate away and got up. "I think I'd better go. Thanks for dinner, Molly." She pushed the chair under the table and left, walking across the courtyard and into the bright sunshine, her knees weak and her eyes full of tears. She waved at Tommy and walked unsteadily to her car.

Liam caught up with her as she was about to drive off. He knocked on the window.

"Open the window," he shouted. "I want to say something to you."

She rolled down the window a couple of inches. "I think you said enough just there."

"I think you misunderstood."

"Did I?" She turned off the engine. "I thought it was pretty clear what you meant."

"No, it wasn't." He turned to Tommy. "Go and wash your hands before we go for ice cream. I'll be with you in a minute." He turned back to Daisy. "Look, I can't talk here. I have to take Tommy for that ice cream. Can we meet later and talk?"

Daisy hesitated. "Not if you're going to give me hell."

Liam glared at her. "Don't be a twit. Can't you see that I'm trying to—" He ran a hand through his hair. "Shit. There's so much I want to say to you, can't you see that?"

"Yes." She could see that. Liam looked frustrated and angry. He just wanted to vent his fury. And who could have blamed him? Being lied to would make anyone feel insulted and cheated.

"I know what you're going to say. But I don't want to hear it. I'm sorry I lied to you. It was a stupid thing to do, okay? But I'm going now. Please don't try to stop me." Tears stinging her eyes, Daisy rolled up the window, started the engine and drove off.

* * *

After parking the car, Daisy let herself into the villa through the garage door in the basement. She punched in the code, walked up the steps to the kitchen area and listened. Not a sound. Not even the usual snuffling and whining from the dogs. She opened the door to their room She opened the door to their room but found it empty. She noticed their leads had disappeared from their hooks and wondered whether Dimitri, whoever he was, was still walking the dogs. But it was late and getting dark. How could he still be out there?

Mystified, Daisy continued to the hall.

"Irina?" she called, her voice echoing up the stairwell. But there was no reply. She opened the door to the office and found it empty. Daisy sat down at the desk and switched on the TV that controlled the security cameras, scanning every room, even the terrace. No sign of life anywhere. Then, just to make sure, she went upstairs and knocked on the door to the master suite. No reply. She slowly opened the door and peered in. Nobody there. Irina's usual disarray of clothes and make-up was missing, and the room looked as empty and pristine as when Daisy had first seen it. Daisy walked across the white carpet and opened the door to the walk-in wardrobe. The rows of designer clothes hung there in exactly the same order as before. But all of Irina's clothes had gone.

Daisy walked around the upstairs bedrooms, then downstairs again, into the living room, through the dining room, the library, down to the kitchen again, into the gym and all the other rooms in turn. Everything was pristine and tidy, as if nobody lived there. She knew then, as if someone had whispered it into her ear, that Irina had left as mysteriously and suddenly as she had arrived. And she had taken the dogs with her. Strange but oddly liberating. Daisy kicked off her shoes and ran upstairs, feeling a huge sense of relief. She would soon be able to leave this weird house and get back to real life. She had to get a message to Belinda to tell her about Irina and the dogs. Then she had to start looking for a new job. She was running away again. Would she ever come to a stop and find a place she could call home?

Deciding to sort everything out the next day, Daisy went into her bedroom to get her swimsuit. An hour in the pool would relax her. But once inside she froze. Despite the room looking like it had that morning when she left, she knew instantly something was wrong. Her clothes, books and personal effects were somehow in a slightly different order. The room had been searched. She ran to the safe and punched in the number to the combination. Looking inside, she saw that everything was still there. Except for her American passport.

* * *

"Gendarmerie de Saint-Tropez, Xavier Bernard à votre service," the voice droned in her ear.

Shit, not him again. But she had to report her stolen passport and then get on to the American consulate.

"Uh, bonjour," Daisy said. "I need to report a stolen passport."

"Very well," Officer Bernard said. "What nationality?"

"American."

"Name?"

"Daisy Hennessy."

"You have the number of your passport?"

"Yes," Daisy said, proud that she had remembered to write it down. She read it out.

"Where was this passport stolen?"

"In the house where I'm staying. Villa Alexandra."

Bernard suddenly sounded more interested. "You had a cambriolage? In your villa?"

"Uh, cambrio—you mean burglary?"

"That is what I mean, yes. Someone broke into your villa?"

"No. I had someone staying here, and now she's gone and I think she stole my passport." In fact, thinking about it, she knew. Irina had planned it all along. That's why she had changed her hair to look more like Daisy. Of course, nobody would have mixed them up, but the passport photo was, like all passport photos, not a good likeness and made her look decidedly shady and years older than she was.

"How do you know this?" Bernard's voice cut into her thoughts.

"I don't. I just assumed." Daisy sighed.

"Assumed. You mean you had a guest who stole from you?"

"No, she wasn't really my guest. Just staying here."

"Her name, please."

"I…oh, forget it," Daisy sighed, exasperated.

"You forgot?" Bernard paused. "If there has been a break-in, we need to come over and look around. That is normal police procedure."

"No! Please don't. There hasn't been a break-in."

"So then your passport is not stolen but lost? You seem to be very forgetful, madame." He paused. "Was it not you who lost a dog some time ago?"

"No, I found a lost dog, but…" Daisy gritted her teeth. "Okay, can we start again? My passport, the number of which I have already told you, has been stolen. I don't quite know when or by whom. That's all I need for you to note down and report to the authorities. Then I will contact the American consulate general and apply for a new passport." She drew breath.

There was a long silence at the other end. Then a sigh. "Très bien, madame. It is now reported. I will send an e-mail to the consulate in Marseille."

"Thank you so much, Officer," Daisy gushed.

"De rien." There was a click as he hung up.

Daisy let out a sigh of relief and looked for the number of the American consulate in Marseille, which had an emergency number for stolen passports. She was told she would have to go in person to apply for a new one, as her current one would be cancelled and anyone trying to use it arrested and questioned. Daisy only felt a tiny dart of guilt that this would get Irina into big trouble, but then she pushed the thought away. The woman deserved to get caught. Who knew what else she had been up to?

* * *

Belinda arrived late in the afternoon the next day, her heels clicking on the hall floor announcing her arrival. Daisy walked down the stairs to greet her.

"Thank you for coming so quickly."

Belinda, looking just as perfect as when they first met, shot her a cold stare. "You're welcome. It's only a four-hour drive from Geneva. I had to come and see what's been going on here."

"Well," Daisy said. "It's a long story. You see, Irina—"

Belinda nodded. "I know all about Mrs Kedrov and that she was here for a while and that she's now gone."

Daisy stared at her. "You know? But how—?"

"Mr Kedrov's people have been keeping an eye on her movements. Except now she seems to have vanished. No sign of her since last night." Belinda opened the door to the office. "Please come in, so we can settle everything."

Daisy walked into the office, where Belinda had started to open the safe. When the door opened, they both stared at the empty space.

"It's empty," Daisy said unnecessarily.

"I can see that," Belinda snapped. "Irina must have taken everything when she left."

"What was in it?"

"Cash, some jewellery and two small Picasso drawings. She must have known the code, after all." Belinda shot Daisy a cold look. "Or you gave it to her."

"I did because she asked me for it. But," Daisy stammered. "Wasn't she entitled? I mean her husband signed the house and its contents to her when they separated, didn't he?"

"No." Belinda sat down behind the desk. "He did not. He gave her some cash and that was all. There was to be a settlement once the divorce was final, but all she was getting was the flat in Moscow. The rest is in his name, including this house."

"Oh." Daisy sank down on the chair. "So she lied to me."

"She must have, yes."

"And she stole my passport."

Belinda's perfectly plucked eyebrows shot up. "Your passport? How stupid of her. But then Irina isn't known for being a genius. If she tries to use it, I'm sure she'll get caught. That's assuming you reported it, of course."

"I reported it last night."

"Good." Belinda checked her phone. "I contacted the police, too. Told them she was here without a visa."

Something occurred to Daisy. "You know, she had a strange kind of boyfriend. And she was always on the computer and talking to him on the phone."

Belinda looked thoughtful. "Hmm. Interesting." She looked at her watch. "Well, we'd better sort everything out then. I have instructions regarding your employment. We want you to stay on here until the date stipulated in your contract even though the dogs appear to have gone missing as well. That's another ten days, is that correct?"

Daisy nodded.

"Good. And then you can leave and confirm by a text

message to me that all is in order. All the codes and locks will be changed after you've left, of course. The house will be sold as soon as it can be arranged. So it would be good if you could be here when the estate agency calls to have a look at the property. They'll want to take photos for a brochure and that sort of thing."

"Sold?" Daisy stared at Belinda. "With everything in it?"

"That's right."

"Even the clothes? I mean the designer clothes in the walk-in wardrobe in the master suite."

Belinda looked confused. "I don't know anything about those. I was ordered by Mr Kedrov to buy them for Irina to wear during the summer season."

"She hated them."

Belinda pursed her lips in a sardonic smile. "Not exactly her style."

"No, that's for sure."

"I'll have to ask Mr Kedrov and his new partner what's to be done with them." Belinda looked at Daisy thoughtfully. "I'm sure, if Mr Kedrov's partner doesn't want them, you could pick out a few things as a thank you for your services. I'll let you know."

Daisy nodded, trying not to look too hopeful. "Thank you. And I'll deal with the real estate agency and help arrange for the photos and all that. I have plenty of experience in that field."

Belinda nodded, looking pleased. "Excellent."

They both jumped as the house phone on the desk rang. Belinda answered.

"Hello? Villa Alexandra. Belinda Fforde speaking." She listened to the voice at the other end and switched to French, her eyes widening and her eyebrows meeting her hairline as she listened. Then she snapped out a string of French, ending with a 'merci' and 'au revoir' and hung up, turning to Daisy. "How extraordinary. That was the police. It appears Irina did indeed try to get to the United States using your passport. She was arrested at Charles de Gaulle in Paris this morning."

"Already? That was quick."

Belinda nodded. "Yes. Apparently, she took the TGV to Paris yesterday and booked the flight straightaway. She was probably trying to use the passport before it was reported stolen. She's being held not only for stealing your passport, but also for trying to smuggle out stolen goods. Items listed in burglaries in this area were found in her luggage. A small Degas bronze and two Van Goghs, among other things."

Daisy's hand flew to her mouth. "Oh my God! So *that's* what she was up to."

Belinda nodded, her mouth in a thin line. "She was involved with a Russian criminal gang based in Berlin. They have operations all over Europe." She shook her head pityingly. "Stupid woman. I'm sure whoever employed her is less than amused. She'll be better off in prison than having to deal with them after this."

Daisy was speechless. But it didn't surprise her. Irina's odd behavior, her whispered conversations on the phone and the questions about security systems all fell into place.

"What about the dogs?" she asked. "What did she do with them?"

Belinda shrugged. "Who knows? She probably parked them with a friend until she could have them shipped. It appears she was planning to stay in the US indefinitely. I have a feeling she was running away from the Russian mafia she was working for."

"Holy shit," Daisy mumbled.

"Indeed." Belinda closed the safe and got up. "That's everything I think." She held out her hand. "Goodbye, Daisy. Thank you for looking after things."

Daisy shook Belinda's hand. "It's been more than a pleasure. The most amazing experience."

Belinda looked surprised. "Really? Was it all the luxury?"

"Partly," Daisy said and turned to the window and the view of the pool and the sea. "But it also opened my eyes to a lot of things."

"But now you're going back to normal life," Belinda remarked.

Daisy turned back to look at Belinda. "No," she said. "I'm not going *back* to anything. I'm going forward"

Chapter 18

Later that evening, as it was Olivier's day off, Daisy went into the kitchen to make a light supper. She quickly gathered together some bread, pâté, cheese, salad and a bottle of rosé. She carried it all to the terrace, where she put it on a table between two loungers. Finally a moment to herself. She realised she hadn't had a chance to think things through and digest the recent events. Even though the last moments with Liam had left a lingering sadness, there was also a feeling of freedom, of being able to plan some kind of future and knowing, at last, what she wanted to do.

She stood for a moment, looking out at the dark, silent landscape. The full moon cast an eerie glow on the lawns and shrubs and made the sea glitter like an undulating diamond-studded carpet. It was still warm and in the lights of the terrace, the turquoise water of the pool looked imminently inviting. Daisy stripped off her shorts and T-shirt. No need for a swimsuit tonight. There was nobody around. First, a swim, then food, followed by some rational thinking.

She sank into the cool water, turned onto her stomach and started to swim, doing a long, slow breaststroke. It was heaven to stretch every muscle and to feel her whole body work after the tension of the day. She breathed in deeply and exhaled, emptying her lungs and her mind with it. She swam two laps, then three, four and five until she lost count and gave herself up to the rhythm of her swimming and the feel of working her body to its limit. When she had enough, she slowed down and turned on her back, looking up at the stars and the moon, enjoying the feel of being weightless, supported by the water. This was heaven. She closed her eyes for a moment and made a wish.

The moment of peace was suddenly interrupted by a splash beside her. Startled, Daisy's head went under the water and she gasped as someone grabbed her by the shoulders. Spluttering and coughing, she managed to get her head above water and fought to free herself of the hands that pulled at her.

They struggled for a moment and then a voice shouted, "Daisy, stop fighting me, I'm trying to help you!"

Daisy pulled away and grabbed the edge of the pool. "Liam? What are you *doing*?"

Liam coughed. "I'm trying to save you, silly woman."

"Save me from what?"

"Killing yourself. I saw you floating there and thought—"

"What?" Daisy lost her grip and nearly sank again but managed to stay afloat.

"I was swimming, you moron," she said when she surfaced. "Then I lay on my back to look at the stars. I was fine until you tried to drown me."

Liam joined her by the edge of the pool. "Shit. Sorry."

"What are you doing here? I thought you loathed me and never wanted to see me again."

"You misunderstood me. Yesterday, I was trying to tell you…but Tommy was there and I couldn't say what was on my mind. You seemed so sad when you left, and you looked at me with such despair."

She turned, let her legs sink and leaned her elbows on the edge, looking out across the garden.

"I was sad. I thought you…" She paused. "That you were disgusted with me for all the lies I've told."

He leaned his chin on his hands, following her gaze. "You

didn't tell lies, exactly. You let people assume you were what you appeared to be."

"Lying by omission, then."

"Well, yes. But who were you hurting? Those people are just as fake. There's stuff going on under the surface of the glitz and glamour you wouldn't believe."

"I think I glimpsed some of it."

"Then you know what I mean." He turned his head and looked at her through the darkness. "You look so beautiful in this light. Your profile is so perfect." He touched her hip under the water. "You're naked."

She moved away. "I thought I was alone. I'm not naked for you. I'm naked for me." She turned to face him. "Can you understand that?"

"Yes. Of course. And I respect that."

"Good."

"Not that it's easy, of course."

"I appreciate that." It wasn't easy for her either, and her body ached with desire to touch him and for him to do what he must be longing to do. She swam further away.

The ensuing silence was charged with emotion. Then he cleared his throat.

"Come on. It's not that bad, is it? So you're not a real princess. I must confess it was a little disappointing. I was going to get you to finance my next movie. I suppose that's out of the question now?"

"Totally," Daisy mumbled, the ghost of a smile on her lips.

He sighed. "Bummer."

"Sorry."

"I'm trying to get over it." He was quiet for a while as he came closer, his legs touching hers under the water as he looked out at the view again. "This is a beautiful place."

"Beautiful and soulless. Empty. Sterile and very lonely."

He glanced at her. "You sound as if you're talking about yourself."

"Maybe I am."

He put his arm around her. "I think we should get out of the water and dry off."

She noticed for the first time that he was wearing his shorts and that he had thrown off his shirt and shoes as he jumped into the pool.

"What are you going to wear? Your shorts are wet."

"If you have a towel, I'll wrap that around me. And if there's a dryer in this mausoleum, you might put my shorts in it for a while."

"Good idea." Daisy swam to the steps, got out of the pool and quickly wrapped a towel around her. She found two white robes in the pool house and after slipping into one of them, handed the other one to Liam. "Give me those shorts and I'll put them in the dryer. There's wine and snacks on the table beside the loungers. I'll get another glass from the kitchen and I'll be back in a minute."

When she came back, Liam, wrapped in the white robe, was already sitting on a lounger, sipping wine. She noticed he had lit the two candles that stood in candleholders on the balustrade. He handed her the glass he had filled and took the empty one. She sat down awkwardly and sipped her wine, hoping it would give her courage.

"Wonderful evening," Liam said. "So warm still."

"Yes," she whispered.

He turned to look at her. "Are you okay?"

"Yes. No. I don't know. There's something odd going on here."

"How do you mean? With us? Or in this house?"

"Both, I suppose." Daisy put her glass on the table. "I should tell you what's been going on."

"Please do."

Daisy pulled her knees up to get more comfortable. "Well, this house belongs to a Russian couple, you see," she started. "I was hired to house-sit and walk the dogs and sort things out with deliveries and so on. It was all fine until that night when I got drunk and you brought me home. The next morning, I found a woman in one of the bedrooms."

"Dead?" Liam exclaimed.

Daisy laughed. "No. This is not one of your thrillers. She was very much alive. She told me that her name was Irina and that she was the wife of the owner but they were splitting up. The owners are Russian, you see."

"Ah. Did she have a problem getting a visa?"

Daisy nodded. "Exactly. Her husband's politics made it very difficult. But Irina managed to get into France and dodge the border police. She had to hide in the house until she could sort out her residency problems. So she was here for about two weeks, stuck in the house, but always in contact with people. Especially one guy called Dimitri. I assumed it was a lover or someone like that. I've no idea what she was really up to. But tonight when I got back here, I found she'd left. There's no trace of her at all. She's just—gone. And she took the dogs with her. Not only that, she stole my American passport."

"Jesus, that's terrible," Liam said, sounding appalled. "What are you going to do?"

"I reported it to the police and the American consulate too. I have to go to Marseille and get a new passport, but there's no rush. I still have my Irish passport."

"Weird," Liam said. "So what happens now? I mean with this job of yours."

Daisy shrugged. "I don't know. Belinda, the woman who hired me, is the PA of the owner. She arrived this afternoon. We were discussing what had happened when the police called to say Irina had been arrested at Charles de Gaulle, trying to use my passport. And she also had some stuff in her luggage that had been stolen in burglaries in this area."

"Bloody hell," Liam said. "So she was involved in all of that?"

"Very much so. It was all done by a Russian crime gang or something, and she was organising some of the thefts. In any case, my term of employment is nearly over. Less than two weeks to go on the contract. So I'll look for another job and then leave." She looked at Liam. "Here I go again. Looking for a job. Story of my life."

He reached over and took her hand. "Not all the story. Not the real, real story, is it?"

"I guess not." There was such comfort in the warmth of his hand. It gave her courage to go on, to tell him everything about herself.

"Go on, then. Tell me."

Daisy took a deep breath. "All right," she said. "You asked for it." Shakily at first, she began to talk. And then little by little she felt more confident. Once she started, she found she couldn't stop, and it all came out in one long thread: her childhood, her dad dying, the horrible years of poverty, the struggle to make a decent living, the love affairs gone bad and finally, Ross.

Liam didn't interrupt her once but kept holding her hand while she talked. When she had finished, he squeezed her hand.

"Thank you. I feel I know you better now. The real Daisy. Not the party princess."

"Yeah, the real me, warts and all," Daisy said and pulled away her hand. "Your turn."

"You want to see my warts?"

"Yes. Everything."

Liam got up and went to sit on the edge of Daisy's lounger. He put his hands on her shoulders. In the dim light of the candles, his eyes were dark and intense.

"I'm not going to tell you the story of my life," he said. "That's for another time. Right now, I just want to say that I'm sorry if I hurt you. The other night was amazing. Then I wrecked it by saying it was some kind of mistake. A shitty thing to say to a woman you've just made love to."

"Yes it was." Daisy blinked away her tears.

"But I didn't mean it. I was scared. Falling in love again seemed so frightening. But then you said that thing about keeping Maureen's memory alive and how I should tell Tommy about his mother. It helped me come to a kind of acceptance. I wanted to tell you, but I didn't know how." He paused and let out a hollow laugh. "I'm a writer, but I still can't find the right words."

Daisy touched his face. "You don't have to say anything. I think I understand. You loved your wife more than your own life. Then you lost her. You'll never forget her, and in a way, you'll always love her. You're scared that if you love someone else, you might lose her too."

He caught her hand. "Something like that. What a coward you must think I am."

"I don't," Daisy protested. "I understand. The truth is, I'm scared too. I don't want to be hurt. I'd rather stay single for the rest of my life than go through that kind of thing again. When I first met you, I thought you were like all the other guys I've had relationships with. So I backed away a little. Except that night. Then I knew, even if I didn't want to admit it to myself."

"Knew what, sweetheart?"

"That I'm in love with you."

He kissed the hand he was holding. "And I'm in love with you. I've known it for quite a long time. Ever since I watched you eat sausages on my patio."

Daisy laughed. "I was such a mess. Grease running down my chin, my mouth full of sausage."

"You were a real woman, a chuisle mo croi."

"You said that to me once before. What does it mean?"

"It's Irish and it means pulse of my heart."

"Oh." Daisy was stunned. "How beautiful." She touched his hair. "You know, my dad used to say about taking risks and daring to love someone, that when you reach for the moon, you'll probably miss, but you might find a star."

"What a wise man he was." Liam moved in beside Daisy and held her tightly. "You want to reach for the moon with me?"

"No need." She put her head on his shoulder. "I think we already found that star."

* * *

Olivier served them breakfast on the terrace the next morning, not showing with even a flicker of an eyelid that he was surprised to find Liam there, dressed in a robe. He simply went back to the kitchen to get another cup and more bread.

"Thank you," Daisy said when he came back. "This is Liam Creedon."

Olivier inclined his head. "We've met once before. Good morning, sir. My name is Olivier. I'm the butler."

"Hi, Olivier. Nice to meet you," Liam said. "Thanks for breakfast."

"You're welcome. Your shorts were still in the dryer when I arrived this morning. I'm afraid they…they're a little frayed."

Daisy clapped her hand over her mouth. "Shit, I forgot about your shorts."

Liam winked at her. "Pants were the last thing on our minds last night, sweetie." He looked at Olivier. "Is there anything left of them? Enough to make me decent, I mean."

"I think so. I'll go and get them." Olivier was about to glide away, but Daisy stopped him.

"You might have noticed that Irina has left."

"Yes. I saw that she also took the dogs." Olivier paused. "But I have been filled in on the situation. Belinda called early this morning. I'll go and get your shorts, sir."

"Great," Daisy said and rolled her eyes after Olivier had left. "He's so discreet, he's nearly invisible. I hope the new owners of the house keep him on. He's so perfect for this place." She sighed and stirred her coffee. "I hope I find a job soon. Don't even know what I want to do."

Liam took her hand. "I'll hire you."

"You haven't seen my résumé."

"I've seen enough to know you'd be perfect."

"As what?"

"As my slave, of course."

"I quit."

Liam laughed. He leaned across the table and kissed her.

"I have to go as soon as I get what's left of my shorts. I have a lot of work piled up."

Daisy nodded. "Yes. I'd better get dressed too and sort things out. Belinda wanted me to contact the interior-design firm and cancel some of the orders. Then the real estate agents will call and set a time for them to come over."

Olivier arrived with Liam's frayed but still wearable shorts. Liam went into the pool house to get dressed. Olivier cleared the breakfast dishes, and Daisy sat down on the edge of the pool, looking out at sea, her mind drifting. She would soon be leaving this beautiful place. Lonely and soulless, yes. But it still had that dreamlike feeling, like a twilight zone, a parallel existence.

It seemed like a whole lifetime since she had arrived that night in June. Since then, so much had happened: the glitz and glamour of the parties; the parading around in designer clothes; Irina's arrival and strange departure; the friendship with Marianne and the work with Molly. All of it crammed into a few weeks. And then falling in love. It didn't seem possible she had at last found someone she truly felt was the love of her life.

She spotted a sail far away on the horizon. Was that Ross? How would he be when he came back? Would she have to hurt him again? But he had seemed so different the last time they met, more confident and determined. Maybe it was possible for them to remain friends after all. But if that wasn't to be, he had to accept it and so did she. No use pouring salt into wounds all the time.

Liam put his hand on her shoulder. "A penny for your thoughts."

She turned and looked up at him, standing there in the bright morning light, the sun shining on his hair and the sea reflected in those brilliant-blue eyes now so full of love.

"I was just going through all the things that have happened during the past few weeks. It all seems like a dream."

"I know." He pulled her up. "But it's real. And now I have to get to work. You have to face the music here and then we can get back on track. And you have to go to Marseille and get a new passport. There's also a lot to do before Molly's launch, and her website needs some tweaking. Then we have to explain to Tommy about us. You're taking on a lot, my sweet. Maybe you should just shake my hand and say 'goodbye, strange to meet you' and run for your life?"

Daisy aimed a playful punch at his jaw. "No way. You'll never be rid of me now."

"I don't want to." He pulled at his shorts. "I'd better hurry home and change before I get arrested. Bye, sweetheart. Let me know when you're ready to move into my old wreck. It'll be a bit of culture shock after the splendour of your current abode."

"I know." Daisy laughed. "Go on, then. Leave. I can't think when you're around."

He kissed her again. "Goodbye, princess."

"Not anymore. I'm just plain old Daisy, remember?"

He touched her cheek. "Plain? Never. You'll always be a princess to me, a chuisle mo croi."

Epilogue

On the morning of Molly's launch, Daisy was woken up at six o'clock by a faint rumbling in the distance. She threw back the bedclothes, padded to the window and opened the shutters, careful not to make a sound. She glanced back at the bed, hoping she hadn't disturbed Liam. But he seemed to be fast asleep, exhausted after working late into the night to meet his deadline.

Daisy had finally left Villa Alexandra a week before the end of her contract. Liam had insisted.

"It's stupid for you to stay on in that mausoleum," he growled. "I want to go to sleep with you beside me and wake up looking at your face. I know I could move in with you there until you leave. But I have to work, and I can't do that in such a sterile place."

It didn't take Daisy more than a second to make up her mind. She e-mailed Belinda and terminated her contract. Belinda replied immediately with a confirmation and full approval. After all, everything was settled, the estate agents had taken their photos, and the house was displayed in their glossy brochure. Belinda also said that she would transfer what was owed to Daisy and that she could take any of the outfits she wanted from the designer collection in the master suite. Daisy picked out the few items she liked the most, leaving the bulk of the collection behind without even the slightest pang of regret. She quickly packed her bags, said a fond farewell to a sad Olivier and left. Her spirits soared when the gates closed behind her, and Liam took her suitcase and loaded them into his dusty Ferrari. She didn't even look back when the car roared up the hill to Villa Mimosa and her new life.

Daisy pushed the shutters further out and peered out at the view of the beach and the bay. She saw black clouds gathering at the horizon, and her heart sank. Thunder. What bad luck. Marianne had planned the launch party in the garden of her beautiful villa. There would be a display of Molly's collection, and Marianne, Daisy and two of Marianne's friends would model the best pieces. It was going to be so perfect there in that lovely garden, with roses and exotic plants displayed against the intense blue of the sea. But as large drops of rain smattered against the roof and windows and the dark clouds rolled even closer, those plans seemed impossible. They would have to do everything indoors. Marianne had laid out a plan B, in case of bad weather, but they had laughed it off. Bad weather on the Riviera? Impossible.

The sound of thunder echoed through the room, followed by the crack and flash of lightning. Daisy took a step back at another clap of thunder, closer this time. She could see forked lightning against the blue-black clouds, lighting up the sea, churned by violent gusts of wind. The rain turned torrential, the sound of thunder more violent. Daisy closed the shutters with a bang and dived under the bedclothes, pulling the blanket over her head.

Liam stirred. "What's the matter?" he mumbled.

"Thunder," Daisy mumbled. "Scary."

Liam wrapped his arms around her. "No need to be scared. This house must have seen thousands of storms during the hundred years or so since it was built. And there's a lightning conductor on the roof. We're perfectly safe."

"Okay," Daisy mumbled against his shoulder. "Hold me tight all the same."

He laughed and squeezed her harder. "Tight enough?"

He was interrupted by the door opening and the sound of feet and claws on the floorboards. Tommy and Asta jumped on the bed and burrowed under the bedclothes. "Thunder," Tommy whimpered. "We're scared."

Daisy made room between herself and Liam. "Here, Tommy. Lie down beside your dad. There's no need to be scared. The thunder can't hurt us."

"It's scary anyway," Tommy mumbled.

Liam put his arm around his son. "I know. The storms can get pretty violent around here."

Daisy got out of bed and pulled on a robe. "I'd better start getting ready. Big day today."

"It's only half past six," Liam protested.

"I know but there's so much to do. I bet Molly's up already. She's probably nervous."

"Yes she is," Tommy said from under the bedclothes. "She's in the kitchen drinking tea. The thunder woke her up too."

Liam said something, but a loud roll of thunder drowned his words. He shrugged and waved his hand at Daisy.

"Go, then, sweetie," he said when the noise had died down. "Tommy and I will be all right. I don't suppose we'll see much of you today."

"Will you come to the launch?"

"Nah, I'll only be a nuisance," Liam grunted. "You and Molly make a great team. You don't need me looking over your shoulder."

"It's a girl thing, Dad said," Tommy piped up.

Daisy laughed. "I bet he did. But it's okay. I really do think he's right this time. "

Liam looked relieved. "Phew."

Tommy popped his head out from under the bedclothes. "Are you going to stay with us, Daisy?"

"Of course," Daisy said.

"Forever?" Tommy asked, looking worried. "I mean like you'll be here tomorrow?"

"You bet," Daisy replied. "And tomorrow and tomorrow and all the tomorrows."

Tommy let out a long sigh. "Good. And good that we don't have to go to your girl party. We're doing something for boys."

"You are? And what would that be?"

"We're going to Azur Park" Tommy said. "And we're doing all the rides."

All the rides?" Liam exclaimed. "If we do half of them I might survive. I'm not doing that roller-coaster death-ride thing and that's final."

Daisy laughed "I'll leave you sort that one out. I have to go run the shower. It takes half an hour to get the water even lukewarm."

"Sorry about that," Liam said. "I'll get it fixed next week. It's just so hard to get a plumber to come this time of year."

"Don't worry," Daisy assured him. "That's a minor problem."

"I'm afraid this old house is a far cry from your previous abode," Liam sighed.

"And thank God for that," Daisy said.

Liam's house certainly was a world away from the luxury of Villa Alexandra, Daisy thought as she stood in the old roll-top bath under the shower. But how comfortable and cared for she felt there, how appreciated and loved and very much a part of this little family. She had been given so many gifts in a short time: the gifts of love and friendship, gifts money couldn't buy.

She even had a budding career as a web designer, even if she was only using basic technique for now. But Liam had urged her to look up online courses in web design and graphics.

"You should do this," he said. "You have a talent for it.

Look what you did with Molly's website. But with no qualifications, you can't start a business and get clients." She agreed and started an online course, which proved to be quite a challenge. There was so much to learn before she could truly call herself a professional.

Daisy dried herself and put her robe back on. She would join Molly for breakfast so they could go through the plan for the day ahead. Her stomach churned as she thought of the launch. It had been her idea. If it failed it would have been all her fault.

* * *

"Fail?" Marianne exclaimed. "It's not going to fail. How can you even contemplate such a thing?"

They were on the terrace of the Villa Farniente, where Marianne had laid out the jewellery on a table covered in dark-blue silk, the perfect background for the different designs and the polished semi-precious stones. The thunder had rolled away out to sea and left behind it bright blue skies and newly washed shrubs and flowers. It would be a perfect day for the launch.

"The display is fabulous," Daisy said. "And so are you. Love what you did to your hair."

"Are you sure?" Marianne patted her hair that had been cut into a short pixie style. "I had about two yards cut off. Klaus nearly fainted."

"Quite a dramatic change, I have to say," Daisy agreed. "And the outfit too." She couldn't take her eyes off Marianne who, in a plain, white, silk T-shirt, skinny jeans and Chanel ballet flats looked like a young girl. Cutting off her light-blonde hair that hung down to her waist had been a brave move that turned Marianne's former Barbie-doll prettiness into a more mature beauty. She looked stunning.

"This is what I like to wear. My new look, not so far from how I used to dress. Very like yours, actually," she said, looking at Daisy's blue shirt, white cotton shorts and flat sandals.

"It's a relief to go back to dressing like a normal person," Daisy remarked.

Marianne giggled. "Just you wait. Everyone will copy us. Jeans and T-shirts will become the new black."

"I wouldn't be a bit surprised. Prada will go out of business." Daisy looked at her watch. "But we have to change. It's eleven o'clock. The photographer will be here in half an hour and Molly's on her way."

"You're right. I'll just get one of the staff to keep an eye on these goodies, and then we can go upstairs to change. Did you bring the cream Chanel dress?"

Daisy held a garment bag aloft. "Right here. One of the items from the collection in the villa. They said I could take whatever I wanted. I picked out three and this one's for the launch."

Marianne nodded her approval. "Fabulous. What's Molly wearing?"

Daisy sighed. "The usual. Peasant skirt, frilly top and about a hundred bangles. I couldn't persuade her to put on something a little more simple and classy."

"But that's great," Marianne argued. "That's totally her. She has to be Molly the designer, not some clone of a model. I love her wild red curls and hippy style. It's very quaint."

"You're right. Stupid of me not to realise it."

"I'm always right," Marianne declared. "But come on. Let's get this show on the road." She started to walk to the door but stopped in her tracks. "Oops, I forgot. There's a letter for you. From Ross."

"A real letter? I haven't heard from him since we had that discussion at the hotel. I thought he might still be angry."

"I think he was out of range for phones or the Internet, so

he posted this letter from Menorca. He sent me a note, too, asking me to forward the letter to you. Go see for yourself. It's on the hall table."

In the dim light of the hall, Daisy read Ross' letter. The message was brief, cheerful and friendly.

Hi Daisy,

Just thought I'd shoot you a note in case you were worried I was still mad at you or upset in any way. I'm not, I swear. During the trip here, to this gorgeous island, I had the chance to do a lot of thinking, as the winds were slack and the weather dull. I was unfair, expecting you to feel what I felt and to fall into bed with me even though you had no desire to do so. You can't order people to love you. I tried and that could have ruined a close friendship. Very wrong of me, I know. But you can't blame a guy for having dreams and fantasies.

I'm going to sail around these islands for a week, and then I'll head home to Antibes, where I have friends and a good life. I'm going to invest in a business with a guy I met recently. He's designing the prototype for a new kind of windsurfing board with double sail capacity. It'll be fun to see where that goes.

In any case, I just wanted you to know all's well. Thank you for your friendship.

All my best wishes, until we meet again.
Ross

Daisy let out a long sigh when she had read the letter.

"Bad news?" Marianne asked.

"No. Good. Nice letter. I just wish he wasn't so goddamn perfect all the time."

Marianne giggled. "I know. He needs to fall in love with some bad girl. Maybe he will one day?"

"I certainly hope so." Daisy stuffed the letter into her bag.

Marianne hovered on her way up the stairs. "And you and Liam? Is he still hot?"

Daisy blushed. "Yeah. We're...I mean...it's incredible. I've never felt like this before."

"Do I hear wedding bells?"

Daisy laughed. "Give us a chance. We only know each other a little over a month. But I have a feeling." She paused. "No, not a feeling. I *know*. This is for real and forever. Liam is the man for me."

"I thought he was too complicated for you at first," Marianne remarked. "Too moody and difficult."

Daisy nodded. "He can be. Very temperamental, like all artists. But he's aware of it and never lets it go too far. And he truly cares about me and how I feel and what I do."

"Wonderful." Marianne was about to start up the stairs but stopped halfway up. "I have something wonderful to tell you too," she said, her eyes shining.

"What?" Daisy squealed. "You're pregnant?"

Marianne laughed. "No, silly. It's about Klaus and me. We're going to Sweden to spend two weeks at my family's cottage on an island outside Stockholm. Just the two of us. At the end of August. No work for him. He just wants to go sailing and swimming and walk barefoot on the rocks and pick blueberries. I couldn't believe it when he said he wanted us to go." She touched her hair. "I think it was my new look. He was mesmerised when he saw it. Couldn't keep his hands off me. Said it was like getting a new wife. Then he asked what would make me happy, so I told him. He said yes immediately."

"That's fabulous," Daisy said, touched by Marianne's shining eyes. "But, hey, we have to get going here and turn ourselves into models. Let's pull out all the stops for Molly."

Laughing, they ran up the stairs to get changed and reappeared half an hour later, all dressed up and glamorous, gliding down the corridor and out onto the terrace where over a hundred guests were waiting. Klaus had volunteered to hold the welcoming speech, which he did with utmost elegance, and the launch was soon in full swing. A blushing Molly arrived a little later to receive applause and accolade for her wonderful work, and the guests practically mobbed her when the modelling session came to an end. Blushing furiously and handing out business cards, Molly did her best to answer their questions. Then she looked at Daisy and smiled, her eyes full of happy tears.

"*Thank you*," she mouthed and then turned back to her new clientele. Daisy let out a long sigh. Molly was well and truly launched.

* * *

High on champagne and the success of the launch, Daisy retired to the guest bedroom where she changed quickly and removed her make-up. She had just packed away her Chanel gown when there was a knock on the door.

"Come in," she called.

The door opened to admit one of Marianne's maids, a sweet girl from Morocco. She smiled shyly. "There is a young man to see you, Mademoiselle."

Daisy blinked. "Who? Oh God, not Ross!"

"No, it's me," Tommy said, skipping into the room with Asta at his heels. "We're here to pick you up and we have a surprise for you."

"A surprise? Did you win something at the amusement park?"

"No. We didn't go there." Tommy took Daisy's hand. "We bought something instead. Come and see." He dragged her to the window. "It's down there, in front of the house. Look."

Daisy looked down at the entrance, but all she could see was a silver hatchback parked in front of the steps.

"What? All I can see is a car."

Tommy laughed. "That's it! That's the surprise. It's a Volvo and it's called a Cross Country V60 and it's our new car."

Daisy looked at Tommy in bewilderment. "But what about the Ferrari?"

"We sold it. We didn't like it anymore. I mean Dad didn't."

Daisy picked up a wriggling Asta from the floor. "Why not? I thought he loved it."

"Not anymore. 'Cause he's stopped being single, he said." Tommy looked up at Daisy. "What's single?"

"It means you're living alone, without being married or dating someone," Daisy explained, the enormity of what had happened slowly dawning on her.

Tommy nodded. "That's it. That's why we need a better car. It's a family car, the man at the garage said. So that fits, doesn't it?"

Daisy looked down at the car and saw Liam getting out of the driver's seat. He looked up at her with a broad smile and waved. She waved back and made a thumbs-up sign.

"Yes, Tommy, it certainly does," she said. "It fits beautifully."

THE END

About the author

Susanne O'Leary is the bestselling author of more than twenty novels, mainly in the romantic fiction genre. She has also written four crime novels and two in the historical fiction genre. She has been the wife of a diplomat (still is), a fitness teacher and a translator. She now writes full-time from either of two locations; a rambling house in County Tipperary, Ireland or a little cottage overlooking the Atlantic in Dingle, County Kerry. When she is not scaling the mountains of said counties, keeping fit in the local gym, or doing yoga, she keeps writing, producing a book every six months.

Find out more about Susanne and her books on her website: http://www.susannne-oleary.co.uk

Made in United States
Troutdale, OR
09/24/2023

13157714R00137